Edgar Wallace was born ⟨…⟩ d
adopted by George Freema⟨…⟩ t
eleven, Wallace sold newsp⟨…⟩ ⟨…⟩
school took a job with a pri⟨…⟩ ⟨…⟩ ⟨…⟩ the Royal West Kent
Regiment, later transferring to the Medical Staff Corps and was sent
to South Africa. In 1898 he published a collection of poems called
The Mission that Failed, left the army and became a correspondent
for Reuters.

Wallace became the South African war correspondent for *The
Daily Mail*. His articles were later published as *Unofficial Dispatches* and
his outspokenness infuriated Kitchener, who banned him as a war
correspondent until the First World War. He edited the *Rand Daily
Mail*, but gambled disastrously on the South African Stock Market,
returning to England to report on crimes and hanging trials. He
became editor of *The Evening News*, then in 1905 founded the Tallis
Press, publishing *Smith*, a collection of soldier stories, and *Four Just
Men*. At various times he worked on *The Standard*, *The Star*, *The Week-
End Racing Supplement* and *The Story Journal*.

In 1917 he became a Special Constable at Lincoln's Inn and also
a special interrogator for the War Office. His first marriage to Ivy
Caldecott, daughter of a missionary, had ended in divorce and he
married his much younger secretary, Violet King.

The Daily Mail sent Wallace to investigate atrocities in the Belgian
Congo, a trip that provided material for his *Sanders of the River* books.
In 1923 he became Chairman of the Press Club and in 1931 stood as
a Liberal candidate at Blackpool. On being offered a scriptwriting
contract at RKO, Wallace went to Hollywood. He died in 1932, on
his way to work on the screenplay for *King Kong*.

Edgar Wallace.

The Angel of Terror

HOUSE OF
STRATUS

This edition published in 2001 by House of Stratus, an imprint of Stratus Holdings plc, 24c Old Burlington Street, London, W1X 1RL, UK.

www.houseofstratus.com

Typeset, printed and bound by House of Stratus.

A catalogue record for this book is available from the British Library.

ISBN 1-84232-658-9

TO
F L S
A MAN OF LAW

1

The hush of the court, which had been broken when the foreman of the jury returned their verdict, was intensified as the Judge, with a quick glance over his pince-nez at the tall prisoner, marshalled his papers with the precision and method which old men display in tense moments such as these. He gathered them together, white paper and blue and buff and stacked them in a neat heap on a tiny ledge to the left of his desk. Then he took his pen and wrote a few words on a printed paper before him.

Another breathless pause and he groped beneath the desk and brought out a small square of black silk and carefully laid it over his white wig. Then he spoke: "James Meredith, you have been convicted after a long and patient trial of the awful crime of wilful murder. With the verdict of the jury I am in complete agreement. There is little doubt, after hearing the evidence of the unfortunate lady to whom you were engaged, and whose evidence you attempted in the most brutal manner to refute, that, instigated by your jealousy, you shot Ferdinand Bulford. The evidence of Miss Briggerland that you had threatened this poor young man, and that you left her presence in a temper, is unshaken. By a terrible coincidence, Mr Bulford was in the street outside your fiancée's door when you left, and maddened by your insane jealousy, you shot him dead.

"To suggest, as you have through your counsel, that you called at Miss Briggerland's that night to break off your engagement and that the interview was a mild one and unattended by recriminations is to suggest that this lady has deliberately committed perjury in order to swear away your life, and when to that disgraceful charge you produce a motive, namely that by your death or imprisonment Miss Briggerland, who is your cousin, would benefit to a considerable extent, you merely add to your infamy. Nobody who saw the young girl in the box, a pathetic, and if I may say, a beautiful figure, could accept for one moment your fantastic explanation.

"Who killed Ferdinand Bulford? A man without an enemy in the world. That tragedy cannot be explained away. It now only remains for me to pass the sentence which the law imposes. The jury's recommendation to mercy will be forwarded to the proper quarter…"

He then proceeded to pass sentence of death, and the tall man in the dock listened without a muscle of his face moving.

So ended the great Berkeley Street Murder Trial, and when a few days later it was announced that the sentence of death had been commuted to one of penal servitude for life, there were newspapers and people who hinted at mistaken leniency and suggested that James Meredith would have been hanged if he were a poor man instead of being, as he was, the master of vast wealth.

"That's that," said Jack Glover between his teeth, as he came out of court with the eminent King's Counsel who had defended his friend and client, "the little lady wins."

His companion looked sideways at him and smiled.

"Honestly, Glover, do you believe that poor girl could do so dastardly a thing as lie about the man she loves?"

"She loves!" repeated Jack Glover witheringly.

"I think you are prejudiced," said the counsel, shaking his head. "Personally, I believe that Meredith is a lunatic; I am satisfied that all he told us about the interview he had with the girl was born of a diseased imagination. I was terribly impressed when I saw Jean Briggerland in the box. She – by Jove, there is the lady!"

They had reached the entrance of the Court. A big car was standing by the kerb and one of the attendants was holding open the door for a girl dressed in black. They had a glimpse of a pale, sad face of extraordinary beauty, and then she disappeared behind the drawn blinds. The counsel drew a long sigh.

"Mad!" he said huskily. "He must be mad! If ever I saw a pure soul in a woman's face, it is in hers!"

"You've been in the sun, Sir John – you're getting sentimental," said Jack Glover brutally, and the eminent lawyer choked indignantly.

Jack Glover had a trick of saying rude things to his friends, even when those friends were twenty years his senior, and by every rule of professional etiquette entitled to respectful treatment.

"Really!" said the outraged Sir John. "There are times, Glover, when you are insufferable!"

But by this time Jack Glover was swinging along the Old Bailey, his hands in his pockets, his silk hat on the back of his head.

He found the grey-haired senior member of the firm of Rennett, Glover and Simpson (there had been no Simpson in the firm for ten years) on the point of going home.

Mr Rennett sat down at the sight of his junior.

"I heard the news by phone," he said. "Elibery says there is no ground for appeal, but I think the recommendation to mercy will save his life – besides it is a *crime passionel*, and they don't hang for homicidal jealousy. I suppose it was the girl's evidence that turned the trick?"

Jack nodded.

"And she looked like an angel just out of the refrigerator," he said despairingly. "Ellbery did his poor best to shake her, but the old fool is half in love with her – I left him raving about her pure soul and her other celestial etceteras."

Mr Rennett stroked his iron grey beard.

"She's won," he said, but the other turned on him with a snarl.

"Not yet!" he said almost harshly. "She hasn't won till Jimmy Meredith is dead or – "

"Or – ?" repeated his partner significantly. "That 'or' won't come off, Jack. He'll get a life sentence as sure as 'eggs is eggs'. I'd go a long way to help Jimmy; I'd risk my practice and my name."

Jack Glover looked at his partner in astonishment.

"You old sportsman!" he said admiringly. "I didn't know you were so fond of Jimmy?"

Mr Rennett got up and began pulling on his gloves. He seemed a little uncomfortable at the sensation he had created.

"His father was my first client," he said apologetically. "One of the best fellows that ever lived. He married late in life, that was why he was such a crank over the question of marriage. You might say that old Meredith founded our firm. Your father and Simpson and I were nearly at our last gasp when Meredith gave us his business. That was our turning point. Your father – God rest him – was never tired of talking about it. I wonder he never told you."

"I think he did," said Jack thoughtfully. "And you really would go a long way – Rennett – I mean, to help Jim Meredith?"

"All the way," said old Rennett shortly.

Jack Glover began whistling a long lugubrious tune.

"I'm seeing the old boy tomorrow," he said. "By the way, Rennett, did you see that a fellow had been released from prison to a nursing home for a minor operation the other day? There was a question asked in Parliament about it. Is it usual?"

"It can be arranged," said Rennett. "Why?"

"Do you think in a few months' time we could get Jim Meredith into a nursing home for – say an appendix operation?"

"Has he appendicitis?" asked the other in surprise.

"He can fake it," said Jack calmly. "It's the easiest thing in the world to fake."

Rennett looked at the other under his heavy eyebrows.

"You're thinking of the 'or'?" he challenged, and Jack nodded.

"It can be done – if he's alive," said Rennett after a pause.

"He'll be alive," prophesied his partner, "now the only thing is – where shall I find the girl?"

2

Lydia Beale gathered up the scraps of paper that littered her table, rolled them into a ball and tossed them into the fire.

There was a knock at the door, and she half turned in her chair to meet with a smile her stout landlady who came in carrying a tray on which stood a large cup of tea and two thick and wholesome slices of bread and jam.

"Finished, Miss Beale?" asked the landlady anxiously.

"For the day, yes," said the girl with a nod, and stood up stretching herself stiffly.

She was slender, a head taller than the dumpy Mrs Morgan. The dark violet eyes and the delicate spiritual face she owed to her Celtic ancestors, the grace of her movements, no less than the perfect hands that rested on the drawing board, spoke eloquently of breed.

"I'd like to see it, miss, if I may," said Mrs Morgan, wiping her hands on her apron in anticipation.

Lydia pulled open a drawer of the table and took out a large sheet of windsor board. She had completed her pencil sketch and Mrs Morgan gasped appreciatively. It was a picture of a masked man holding a villainous crowd at bay at the point of a pistol.

"That's wonderful, miss," she said in awe. "I suppose those sort of things happen too?"

The girl laughed as she put the drawing away.

"They happen in stories which I illustrate, Mrs Morgan," she said dryly. "The real brigands of life come in the shape of lawyers' clerks with writs and summonses. It's a relief from those mad fashion plates

I draw, anyway. Do you know, Mrs Morgan, that the sight of a dressmaker's shop window makes me positively ill!"

Mrs Morgan shook her head sympathetically and Lydia changed the subject.

"Has anybody been this afternoon?" she asked.

"Only the young man from Spadd & Newton," replied the stout woman with a sigh. "I told 'im you was out, but I'm a bad liar."

The girl groaned.

"I wonder if I shall ever get to the end of those debts," she said in despair. "I've enough writs in the drawer to paper the house, Mrs Morgan."

Three years ago Lydia Beale's father had died and she had lost the best friend and companion that any girl ever had. She knew he was in debt, but had no idea how extensively he was involved. A creditor had seen her the day after the funeral and had made some uncouth reference to the convenience of a death which had automatically cancelled George Beale's obligations. It needed only that to spur the girl to an action which was as foolish as it was generous. She had written to all the people to whom her father owed money and had assumed full responsibility for debts amounting to hundreds of pounds.

It was the Celt in her that drove her to shoulder the burden which she was ill-equipped to carry, but she had never regretted her impetuous act.

There were a few creditors who, realising what had happened, did not bother her, and there were others...

She earned a fairly good salary on the staff of the *Daily Megaphone*, which made a feature of fashion, but she would have had to have been the recipient of a Cabinet minister's emoluments to have met the demands which flowed in upon her a month after she had accepted her father's obligations.

"Are you going out tonight, miss?" asked the woman.

Lydia roused herself from her unpleasant thoughts.

"Yes. I'm making some drawings of the dresses in Curfew's new play. I'll be home somewhere around twelve."

Mrs Morgan was halfway across the room when she turned back.

"One of these days you'll get out of all your troubles, miss, you see if you don't! I'll bet you'll marry a rich young gentleman."

Lydia, sitting on the edge of the table, laughed.

"You'd lose your money, Mrs Morgan," she said, "rich young gentlemen only marry poor working girls in the kind of stories I illustrate. If I marry it will probably be a very poor young gentleman who will become an incurable invalid and want nursing. And I shall hate him so much that I can't be happy with him, and pity him so much that I can't run away from him."

Mrs Morgan sniffed her disagreement.

"There are things that happen – " she began.

"Not to me – not miracles, anyway," said Lydia, still smiling, "and I don't know that I want to get married. I've got to pay all these bills first, and by the time they are settled I'll be a grey-haired old lady in a mob cap."

Lydia had finished her tea and was standing somewhat scantily attired in the middle of her bedroom, preparing for her theatre engagement, when Mrs Morgan returned.

"I forgot to tell you, miss," she said, "there was a gentleman and a lady called."

"A gentleman and a lady? Who were they?"

"I don't know, Miss Beale. I was lying down at the time, and the girl answered the door. I gave her strict orders to say that you were out."

"Did they leave any name?"

"No, miss. They just asked if Miss Beale lived here, and could they see her."

"H'm!" said Lydia with a frown. "I wonder what we owe them!"

She dismissed the matter from her mind, and thought no more of it until she stopped on her way to the theatre to learn from the office by telephone the number of drawings required.

The chief sub-editor answered her.

"And, by the way," he added, "there was an inquiry for you at the office today – I found a note of it on my desk when I came in tonight.

Some old friends of yours who want to see you. Brand told them you were going to do a show at the Erving Theatre tonight, so you'll probably see them."

"Who are they?" she asked, puzzled.

She had few friends, old or new.

"I haven't the foggiest idea," was the reply.

At the theatre she saw nobody she knew, though she looked round interestedly, nor was she approached in any of the *entr'actes*.

In the row ahead of her, and a little to her right, were two people who regarded her curiously as she entered. The man was about fifty, very dark and bald – the skin of his head was almost copper-coloured, though he was obviously a European, for the eyes which beamed benevolently upon her through powerful spectacles were blue, but so light a blue that by contrast with the mahogany skin of his clean-shaven face, they seemed almost white.

The girl who sat with him was fair, and to Lydia's artistic eye, singularly lovely. Her hair was a mop of fine gold. The colour was natural, Lydia was too sophisticated to make any mistake about that. Her features were regular and flawless. The young artist thought she had never seen so perfect a "cupid" mouth in her life. There was something so freshly, fragrantly innocent about the girl that Lydia's heart went out to her, and she could hardly keep her eyes on the stage. The unknown seemed to take almost as much interest in her, for twice Lydia surprised her backward scrutiny. She found herself wondering who she was. The girl was beautifully dressed, and about her neck was a platinum chain that must have hung to her waist – a chain which was broken every few inches by a big emerald.

It required something of an effort of concentration to bring her mind back to the stage and her work. With a book on her knee she sketched the somewhat bizarre costumes which had aroused a mild public interest in the play, and for the moment forgot her entrancing companion.

She came through the vestibule at the end of the performance, and drew her worn cloak more closely about her slender shoulders, for the night was raw, and a sou'westerly wind blew the big wet snowflakes under the protecting glass awning into the lobby itself. The favoured playgoers minced daintily through the slush to their waiting cars, then taxis came into the procession of waiting vehicles, there was a banging of cab doors, a babble of orders to the scurrying attendants, until something like order was evolved from the chaos.

"Cab, miss?"

Lydia shook her head. An omnibus would take her to Fleet Street, but two had passed, packed with passengers, and she was beginning to despair, when a particularly handsome taxi pulled up at the kerb.

The driver leant over the shining apron which partially protected him from the weather, and shouted: "Is Miss Beale there?"

The girl started in surprise, taking a step toward the cab.

"I am Miss Beale," she said.

"Your editor has sent me for you," said the man briskly.

The editor of the *Megaphone* had been guilty of many eccentric acts. He had expressed views on her drawing which she shivered to recall. He had aroused her in the middle of the night to sketch dresses at a fancy dress ball, but never before had he done anything so human as to send a taxi for her. Nevertheless, she would not look at the gift cab too closely, and she stepped into the warm interior.

The windows were veiled with the snow and the sleet which had been falling all the time she had been in the theatre. She saw blurred lights flash past, and realised that the taxi was going at a good pace. She rubbed the windows and tried to look out after a while. Then she endeavoured to lower one, but without success. Suddenly she jumped up and tapped furiously at the window to attract the driver's attention. There was no mistaking the fact that they were crossing a bridge and it was not necessary to cross a bridge to reach Fleet Street.

If the driver heard he took no notice. The speed of the car increased. She tapped at the window again furiously. She was not afraid, but she was angry. Presently fear came. It was when she tried to open the door, and found that it was fastened from the outside, that she struck a match to discover that the windows had been screwed tight – the edge of the hole where the screw had gone in was rawly new, and the screw's head was bright and shining.

She had no umbrella – she never carried one to the theatre – and nothing more substantial in the shape of a weapon than a fountain pen. She could smash the windows with her foot. She sat back in the seat, and discovered that it was not so easy an operation as she had thought. She hesitated even to make the attempt; and then the panic sense left her, and she was her own calm self again. She was not being abducted. These things did not happen in the twentieth century, except in sensational books. She frowned. She had said almost the same thing to somebody that day – to Mrs Morgan, who had hinted at a romantic marriage. Of course, nothing was wrong. The driver had called her by name. Probably the editor wanted to see her at his home, he lived somewhere in South London, she remembered. That would explain everything. And yet her instinct told her that something unusual was happening, that some unpleasant experience was imminent.

She tried to put the thought out of her mind, but it was too vivid, too insistent.

Again she tried the door, and then, conscious of a faint reflected glow on the cloth-lined roof of the cab, she looked backward through the peephole. She saw two great motor-car lamps within a few yards of the cab. A car was following, she glimpsed the outline of it as they ran past a street standard.

They were in one of the roads of the outer suburbs. Looking through the window over the driver's shoulder she saw trees on one side of the road, and a long grey fence. It was while she was so looking that the car behind shot suddenly past and ahead, and she saw its tail lights moving away with a pang of hopelessness. Then, before she realised what had happened, the big car ahead slowed and swung sideways, blocking the road, and the cab came to a jerky stop that flung her against the window. She saw two figures in the dim light of the taxi's headlamps, heard somebody speak, and the door was jerked open.

"Will you step out, Miss Beale," said a pleasant voice, and though her legs seemed queerly weak, she obliged. The second man was standing by the side of the driver. He wore a long raincoat, the collar of which was turned up to the tip of his nose.

"You may go back to your friends and tell them that Miss Beale is in good hands," he was saying. "You may also burn a candle or two before your favourite saint, in thanksgiving that you are alive."

"I don't know what you're talking about," said the driver sulkily. "I'm taking this young lady to her office."

"Since when has the *Daily Megaphone* been published in the ghastly suburbs?" asked the other politely.

He saw the girl, and raised his hat. "Come along, Miss Beale," he said. "I promise you a more comfortable ride – even if I cannot guarantee that the end will be less startling."

3

The man who had opened the door was a short, stoutly built person of middle age. He took the girl's arm gently, and without questioning she accompanied him to the car ahead, the man in the raincoat following. No word was spoken, and Lydia was too bewildered to ask questions until the car was on its way. Then the younger man chuckled.

"Clever, Rennett!" he said. "I tell you, those people are super-humanly brilliant!"

"I'm not a great admirer of villainy," said the other gruffly, and the younger man, who was sitting opposite the girl, laughed.

"You must take a detached interest, my dear chap. Personally, I admire them. I admit they gave me a fright when I realised that Miss Beale had not called the cab, but that it had been carefully planted for her, but still I can admire them."

"What does it mean?" asked the puzzled girl. "I'm so confused – where are we going now? To the office?"

"I fear you will not get to the office tonight," said the young man calmly, "and it is impossible to explain to you just why you were abducted."

"Abducted?" said the girl incredulously. "Do you mean to say that man – "

"He was carrying you into the country," said the other calmly. "He would probably have travelled all night and have left you stranded in some unget-at-able place. I don't think he meant any harm – they never take unnecessary risks, and all they wanted was to spirit you away for the night. How they came to know that we had chosen you baffles me," he said. "Can you advance any theory, Rennett?"

"Chosen me?" repeated the startled girl. "Really, I feel I'm entitled to some explanation, and if you don't mind, I would like you to take me back to my office. I have a job to keep," she added grimly.

"Six pounds ten a week, and a few guineas extra for your illustrations," said the man in the raincoat. "Believe me, Miss Beale, you'll never pay off your debts on that salary, not if you live to be a hundred."

She could only gasp.

"You seem to know a great deal about my private affairs," she said, when she had recovered her breath.

"A great deal more than you can imagine."

She guessed he was smiling in the darkness, and his voice was so gentle and apologetic that she could not take offence.

"In the past twelve months you have had thirty-nine judgments recorded against you, and in the previous year, twenty-seven. You are living on exactly thirty shillings a week, and all the rest is going to your father's creditors."

"You're very impertinent!" she said hotly and, as she felt, foolishly.

"I'm very pertinent, really. By the way, my name is Glover – John Glover, of the firm of Rennett, Glover and Simpson. The gentleman at your side is Mr Charles Rennett, my senior partner. We are a firm of solicitors, but how long we shall remain a firm," he added pointedly, "depends rather upon you."

"Upon me?" said the girl in genuine astonishment. "Well, I can't say that I have so much love for lawyers – "

"That I can well understand," murmured Mr Glover.

"But I certainly do not wish to dissolve your partnership," she went on.

"It is rather more serious than that," said Mr Rennett, who was sitting by her side. "The fact is, Miss Beale, we are acting in a perfectly illegal manner, and we are going to reveal to you the particulars of an act we contemplate, which, if you pass on the information to the police, will result in our professional ruin. So you see this adventure is infinitely more important to us than at present it is to you. And here we are!" he said, interrupting the girl's question.

The car turned into a narrow drive, and proceeded some distance through an avenue of trees before it pulled up at the pillared porch of a big house.

Rennett helped her to alight and ushered her through the door, which opened almost as they stopped, into a large panelled hall.

"This is the way, let me show you," said the younger man.

He opened a door and she found herself in a big drawing-room, exquisitely furnished and lit by two silver electroliers suspended from the carved roof.

To her relief an elderly woman rose to greet her.

"This is my wife, Miss Beale," said Rennett. "I need hardly explain that this is also my home."

"So you found the young lady," said the elderly lady, smiling her welcome, "and what does Miss Beale think of your proposition?"

The young man Glover came in at that moment, and divested of his long raincoat and hat, he proved to be of a type that the Universities turn out by the hundred. He was good-looking too, Lydia noticed with feminine inconsequence, and there was something in his eyes that inspired trust. He nodded with a smile to Mrs Rennett, then turned to the girl.

"Now Miss Beale, I don't know whether I ought to explain or whether my learned and distinguished friend prefers to save me the trouble."

"Not me," said the elder man hastily. "My dear," he turned to his wife, "I think we'll leave Jack Glover to talk to this young lady."

"Doesn't she know?" asked Mrs Rennett in surprise, and Lydia laughed, although she was feeling far from amused.

The possible loss of her employment, the disquieting adventure of the evening, and now this further mystery all combined to set her nerves on edge.

Glover waited until the door closed on his partner and his wife and seemed inclined to wait a little longer, for he stood with his back to the fire, biting his lips and looking down thoughtfully at the carpet.

"I don't just know how to begin, Miss Beale," he said. "And having seen you, my conscience is beginning to work overtime. But I might as well start at the beginning. I suppose you have heard of the Bulford murder?"

The girl stared at him.

"The Bulford murder?" she said incredulously, and he nodded.

"Why, of course, everybody has heard of that."

"Then happily it is unnecessary to explain all the circumstances," said Jack Glover, with a little grimace of distaste.

"I only know," interrupted the girl, "that Mr Bulford was killed by a Mr Meredith, who was jealous of him, and that Mr Meredith, when he went into the witness box, behaved disgracefully to his fiancée."

"Exactly," nodded Glover with a twinkle in his eye. "In other words, he repudiated the suggestion that he was jealous, swore that he had already told Miss Briggerland that he could not marry her, and he did not even know that Bulford was paying attention to the lady."

"He did that to save his life," said Lydia quietly. "Miss Briggerland swore in the witness box that no such interview had occurred."

Glover nodded.

"What you do not know, Miss Beale," he said gravely, "is that Jean Briggerland was Meredith's cousin, and unless certain things happen, she will inherit the greater part of six hundred thousand pounds from Meredith's estate. Meredith, I might explain, is one of my best friends, and the fact that he is now serving out a life sentence does not make him any less a friend. I am as sure, as I am sure of your sitting there, that he no more killed Bulford than I did. I believe the whole thing was a plot to secure his death or imprisonment. My partner thinks the same. The truth is that Meredith was engaged to this girl; he discovered certain things about her and her father which are not greatly to their credit. He was never really in love with her, beautiful as she is, and he was trapped into the proposal. When he found out how things were shaping and heard some of the queer stories which were told about Briggerland and his daughter, he broke off the engagement and went that night to tell her so."

The girl had listened in some bewilderment to this recital.

15

"I don't exactly see what all this is to do with me," she said, and again Jack Glover nodded.

"I can quite understand," he said, "but I will tell you yet another part of the story which is not public property. Meredith's father was an eccentric man who believed in early marriages, and it was a condition of his will that if Meredith was not married by his thirtieth birthday, the money should go to his sister, her heirs and successors. His sister was Mrs Briggerland, who is now dead. Her heirs are her husband and Jean Briggerland."

There was a silence. The girl stared thoughtfully into the fire.

"How old is Mr Meredith?"

"He is thirty next Monday," said Glover quietly, "and it is necessary that he should be married before next Monday."

"In prison?" she asked.

He shook his head.

"If such things are allowed that could have been arranged, but for some reason the Home Secretary refuses to exercise his discretion in this matter, and has resolutely refused to allow such a marriage to take place. He objects on the ground of public policy, and I dare say from his point of view he is right. Meredith has a twenty-year sentence to serve."

"Then how – " began Lydia.

"Let me tell this story more or less understandably," said Glover with that little smile of his. "Believe me, Miss Beale, I'm not so keen upon the scheme as I was. If by chance," he spoke deliberately, "we could get James Meredith into this house tomorrow morning, would you marry him?"

"Me?" she gasped. "Marry a man I've not seen – a murderer?"

"Not a murderer," he said gently.

"But it is preposterous, impossible!" she protested. "Why me?"

He was silent for a moment.

"When this scheme was mooted we looked round for someone to whom such a marriage would be of advantage," he said, speaking slowly. "It was Rennett's idea that we should search the County Court records of London to discover if there was a girl who was in urgent

16

need of money. There is no surer way of unearthing financial skeletons than by searching County Court records. We found four, only one of whom was eligible and that was you. Don't interrupt me for a moment, please," he said, raising his hand warningly as she was about to speak. "We have made thorough inquiries about you, too thorough in fact, because the Briggerlands have smelt a rat, and have been on our trail for a week. We know that you are not engaged to be married, we know that you have a fairly heavy burden of debts, and we know, too, that you are unencumbered by relations or friends. What we offer you, Miss Beale, and believe me I feel rather a cad in being the medium through which the offer is made, is five thousand pounds a year for the rest of your life, a sum of twenty thousand pounds down, and the assurance that you will not be troubled by your husband from the moment you are married."

Lydia listened like one in a dream. It did not seem real. She would wake up presently and find Mrs Morgan with a cup of tea in her hand and a plate of her indigestible cakes. Such things did not happen, she told herself, and yet here was a young man, standing with his back to the fire, explaining in the most commonplace conversational tone, an offer which belonged strictly to the realm of romance, and not too convincing romance at that.

"You've rather taken my breath away," she said after a while. "All this wants thinking about, and if Mr Meredith is in prison – "

"Mr Meredith is not in prison," said Glover quietly. "He was released two days ago to go to a nursing home for a slight operation. He escaped from the nursing home last night and at this particular moment is in this house."

She could only stare at him open-mouthed, and he went on.

"The Briggerlands know he has escaped; they probably thought he was here, because we have had a police visitation this afternoon, and the interior of the house and grounds have been searched. They know, of course, that Mr Rennett and I were his legal advisers, and we expected them to come. How he escaped their observation is neither here nor there. Now, Miss Beale, what do you say?"

"I don't know what to say," she said, shaking her head helplessly. "I know I'm dreaming, and if I had the moral courage to pinch myself hard, I should wake up. Somehow I don't want to wake, it is so fascinatingly impossible."

He smiled.

"Can I see Mr Meredith?"

"Not till tomorrow. I might say that we've made every arrangement for your wedding, the licence has been secured and at eight o'clock tomorrow morning – marriages before eight or after three are not legal in this country, by the way – a clergyman will attend and the ceremony will be performed."

There was a long silence.

Lydia sat on the edge of her chair, her elbows on her knees, her face in her hands.

Glover looked down at her seriously, pityingly, cursing himself that he was the exponent of his own grotesque scheme. Presently she looked up.

"I think I will," she said a little wearily. "And you were wrong about the number of judgment summonses, there were seventy-five in two years – and I'm so tired of lawyers."

"Thank you," said Jack Glover politely.

4

All night long she had sat in the little bedroom to which Mrs Rennett had led her, thinking and thinking and thinking. She could not sleep, although she had tried hard, and most of the night she spent pacing up and down from window to door turning over the amazing situation in which she found herself. She had never thought of marriage seriously, and really a marriage such as this presented no terrors and might, had the prelude been a little less exciting, been accepted by her with relief. The prospect of being a wife in name only, even the thought that her husband would be, for the next twenty years, behind prison walls, neither distressed nor horrified her. Somehow she accepted Glover's statement that Meredith was innocent, without reservation.

She wondered what Mrs Morgan would say and what explanation she would give at the office. She was not particularly in love with her work, and it would be no wrench for her to drop it and give herself up to the serious study of art. Five thousand pounds a year! She could live in Italy, study under the best masters, have a car of her own – the possibilities seemed illimitable – and the disadvantages?

She shrugged her shoulders as she answered the question for the twentieth time. What disadvantages were there? She could not marry, but then she did not want to marry. She was not the kind to fall in love, she told herself, she was too independent, too sophisticated, and understood men and their weaknesses only too well.

"The Lord designed me for an old maid," she said to herself.

At seven o'clock in the morning – a grey, cheerless morning it was, thought Lydia, looking out of the window – Mrs Rennett came in with some tea.

"I'm afraid you haven't slept, my dear," she said with a glance at the bed. "It's very trying for you."

She laid her hand upon the girl's arm and squeezed it gently.

"And it's very trying for all of us," she said with a whimsical smile. "I expect we shall all get into fearful trouble."

That had occurred to the girl too, remembering the gloomy picture which Glover had painted in the car.

"Won't this be very serious for you, if the authorities find that you have connived at the escape?" she asked.

"Escape, my dear?" Mrs Rennett's face became a mask. "I have not heard anything of an escape. All that we know is that poor Mr Meredith, anticipating that the Home Office would allow him to get married, had made arrangements for the marriage at this house. How Mr Meredith comes here is quite a matter outside our knowledge," said the diplomatic lady, and Lydia laughed in spite of herself.

She spent half an hour making herself presentable for the forthcoming ordeal.

As a church clock struck eight, there came another tap on the door. It was Mrs Rennett again.

"They are waiting," she said. Her face was a little pale and her lips trembled.

Lydia, however, was calmness itself, as she walked into the drawing-room ahead of her hostess.

There were four men. Glover and Rennett she knew. A third man wearing a clerical collar she guessed was the officiating priest, and all her attention was concentrated upon the fourth. He was a gaunt, unshaven man, his hair cut short, his face and figure wasted, so that the clothes he wore hung on him. Her first feeling was one of revulsion. Her second was an impulse of pity. James Meredith, for she guessed it was he, appeared wretchedly ill. He swung round as she came in, and looked at her intently, then, walking quickly towards her, he held out his thin hand.

"Miss Beale, isn't it?" he said. "I'm sorry to meet you under such unpleasant circumstances. Glover has explained everything, has he not?"

She nodded.

His deep-set eyes had a magnetic quality that fascinated her.

"You understand the terms? Glover has told you just why this marriage must take place?" he said, lowering his voice. "Believe me, I am deeply grateful to you for falling in with my wishes."

Without preliminary he walked over to where the parson stood.

"We will begin now," he said simply.

The ceremony seemed so unreal to the girl that she did not realise what it portended, not even when a ring (a loosely-fitting ring, for Jack Glover had made the wildest guess at the size) was slipped over her finger. She knelt to receive the solemn benediction and then got slowly to her feet and looked at her husband strangely.

"I think I'm going to faint," she said.

It was Jack Glover who caught her and carried her to the sofa. She woke with a confused idea that somebody was trying to hypnotise her, and she opened her eyes to look upon the sombre face of James Meredith.

"Better?" he asked anxiously. "I'm afraid you've had a trying time, and no sleep you said, Mrs Rennett?"

Mrs Rennett shook her head.

"Well, you'll sleep tonight better than I shall," he smiled, and then he turned to Rennett, a grave and anxious man, who stood nervously stroking his little beard, watching the bridegroom. "Mr Rennett," he said, "I must tell you in the presence of witnesses, that I have escaped from a nursing home to which I had been sent by the clemency of the Secretary of State. When I informed you that I had received permission to come to your house this morning to get married, I told you that which was not true."

21

"I'm sorry to hear that," said Rennett politely. "And, of course, it is my duty to hand you over to the police, Mr Meredith."

It was all part of the game. The girl watched the play, knowing that this scene was carefully rehearsed, in order to absolve Rennett and his partner from complicity in the escape.

Rennett had hardly spoken when there was a loud rat-tat at the front door, and Jack Glover hastened into the hall to answer. But it was not the policeman he had expected. It was a girl in a big sable coat, muffled up to her eyes. She pushed past Jack, crossed the hall, and walked straight into the drawing-room.

Lydia, standing shakily by Mrs Rennett's side, saw the visitor come in, and then, as she unfastened her coat, recognised her with a gasp. It was the beautiful girl she had seen in the stalls of the theatre the night before! "And what can we do for you?" It was Glover's voice again, bland and bantering.

"I want Meredith," said the girl shortly, and Glover chuckled.

"You have wanted Meredith for a long time, Miss Briggerland," he said, "and you're likely to want. You have arrived just a little too late."

The girl's eyes fell upon the parson.

"Too late," she said slowly, "then he is married?"

She bit her red lips and nodded, then she looked at Lydia, and the blue eyes were expressionless.

Meredith had disappeared. Lydia looked round for him in her distress, but he had gone. She wondered if he had gone out to the police, to make his surrender, and she was still wondering when there came the sound of a shot.

It was from the outside of the house, and at the sound Glover ran through the doorway, crossed the hall and flew into the open. It was still snowing, and there was no sign of any human being. He raced along a path which ran parallel with the house, turned the corner and dived into a shrubbery. Here the snow had not laid, and he followed the garden path that twisted and turned through the thick laurel bushes and ended at a roughly built tool house. As he came in sight of the shed he stopped.

A man lay on the ground, his arm extended, his head in a pool of blood, his grey hand clutching a revolver.

Jack uttered an exclamation of horror and ran to the side of the fallen man.

It was James Meredith, and he was dead.

5

Jack Glover heard footsteps coming down the path, and turned to meet a man who had "detective" written largely all over him. Jack turned and looked down again at the body as the man came up.

"Who is this?" asked the officer sharply. "It is James Meredith," said Jack simply. "Dead?" said the officer, startled. "He has committed suicide!"

Jack did not reply, and watched the inspector as he made his brief, quick examination of the body. A bullet had entered just below the left temple, and there was a mark of powder near the face.

"A very bad business, Mr Glover," said the police officer seriously. "Can you account for this man being here?"

"He came to get married," said Jack listlessly. "I dare say that startles you, but it is the fact. He was married less than ten minutes ago. If you will come up to the house I will explain his presence here."

The detective hesitated, but just then another of his comrades came on the scene, and Jack led the way back to the house through a back door into Rennett's study.

The lawyer was waiting for them, and he was alone.

"If I'm not very much mistaken, you're Inspector Colhead, of Scotland Yard," said Glover.

"That is my name," nodded the officer. "Between ourselves, Mr Glover, I don't think I should make any statement which you are not prepared to verify publicly."

Jack noted the significance of the warning with a little smile, and proceeded to tell the story of the wedding.

"I can only tell you," he said in answer to a further inquiry, "that Mr Meredith came into this house at a quarter to eight this morning, and surrendered himself to my partner. At eight o'clock exactly, as you are well aware, Mr Rennett telephoned to Scotland Yard to say that Mr Meredith was here. During the period of his waiting he was married."

"Did a parson happen to be staying here, sir?" asked the police officer sarcastically.

"He happened to be staying here," said Jack calmly, "because I had arranged for him to be here. I knew that if it was humanly possible, Mr Meredith would come to this house, and that his desire was to be married, for reasons which my partner will explain."

"Did you help him to escape? That is asking you a leading question," smiled the detective.

Jack shook his head.

"I can answer you with perfect truth that I did not, any more than the Home Secretary helped him when he gave him permission to go to a nursing home."

Soon after the detective returned to the shed, and Jack and his partner were left alone.

"Well?" said Rennett, in a shaking voice, "what happened?"

"He's dead," said Jack quietly.

"Suicide?"

Jack looked at him oddly.

"Did Bulford commit suicide?" he asked.

"Where is the angel?"

"I left her in the drawing-room with Mrs Rennett and Miss Beale."

"Mrs Meredith," corrected Jack quietly.

"This complicates matters," said Rennett, "but I think we can get out of our share of the trouble, though it is going to look a little black."

They found the three women in the drawing-room. Lydia, looking very white, came to meet them.

"What happened?" she asked, and then she guessed from his face. "He's not dead?" she gasped.

Jack nodded. All the time his eyes were on the other girl. Her beautiful lips were drooped a little. There was a look of pain and sorrow in her eyes that caught his breath.

"Did he shoot himself?" she asked in a low voice.

Jack regarded her coldly.

"The only thing that I am certain about," and Lydia winced at the cruelty in his voice, "is that you did not shoot him, Miss Briggerland."

"How dare you!" flamed Jean Briggerland. The quick flush that came to her cheek was the only other evidence of emotion she betrayed.

"I dare say a lot," said Jack curtly. "You asked me if it is a case of suicide, and I tell you that it is not – it is a case of murder. James Meredith was found with a revolver clutched in his right hand. He was shot through the left temple, and if you'll explain to me how any man, holding a pistol in a normal way, can perform that feat, I will accept your theory of suicide."

There was a dead silence.

"Besides," Jack went on, with a little shrug, "poor Jimmy had no pistol."

Jean Briggerland had dropped her eyes, and stood there with downcast head and compressed lips. Presently she looked up.

"I know how you feel, Mr Glover," she said gently. "I can well understand, believing such dreadful things about me as you do, that you must hate me."

Her mouth quivered and her voice grew husky with sorrow.

"I loved James Meredith," she said, "and he loved me."

"He loved you well enough to marry somebody else," said Jack Glover, and Lydia was shocked.

"Mr Glover," she said reproachfully, "do you think it is right to say these things, with poor Mr Meredith lying dead?"

He turned slowly toward her, and she saw in his humorous eyes a hardness that she had not seen before.

"Miss Briggerland has told us that I hate her," he said in an even voice, "and she spoke nothing but the truth. I hate her perhaps beyond understanding – Mrs Meredith." He emphasised the words, and the girl winced. "And one day, if the Circumstantialists spare me – "

"The Circumstantialists" said Jean Briggerland slowly. "I don't quite understand you."

Jack Glover laughed, and it was not a pleasant laugh.

"Perhaps you will," he said shortly. "As to your loving poor Jim – well, you know best. I am trying to be polite to you, Miss Briggerland, and not to gloat over the fact that you arrived too late to stop this wedding! And shall I tell you why you arrived too late?" His eyes were laughing again. "It was because I had arranged with the vicar of St Peter's to be here at nine o'clock this morning, well knowing that you and your little army of spies would discover the hour of the wedding, and would take care to be here before. And then I secretly sent for an old Oxford friend of mine to be here at eight – he was here last night."

Still she stood regarding him without visible evidence of the anger which Lydia thought would have been justified.

"I had no desire to stop the wedding," said the girl, in a low, soft voice. "If Jim preferred to be married in this way to somebody who does not know him, I can only accept his choice." She turned to the girl and held out her hand. "I am very sorry that this tragedy has come to you, Mrs Meredith," she said. "May I wish you a greater happiness than any you have found?"

Lydia was touched by the sincerity, hurt a little by Glover's uncouthness, and could only warmly grip the little hand that was held out to her.

"I'm sorry too," she said a little unsteadily. "For you more than for – anything else."

The girl lowered her eyes and again her lips quivered, and then without a word she walked out of the room, pulling her sable wrap about her throat.

It was noon before Rennett's car deposited Lydia Meredith at the door of her lodging.

She found Mrs Morgan in a great state of anxiety, and the stout little woman almost shed tears of joy at the sight of her.

"Oh, miss, you've no idea how worried I've been," she babbled, "and they've been round here from your newspaper office asking where you are. I thought you had been run over or something, and the *Daily Megaphone* have sent to all the hospitals – "

"I have been run over," said Lydia wearily. "My poor mind has been under the wheels of a dozen motorbuses, and my soul has been in a hundred collisions."

Mrs Morgan gaped at her. She had no sense of metaphor.

"It's all right, Mrs Morgan," laughed her lodger over her shoulder as she went up the stairs. "I haven't really, you know, only I've had a worrying time – and by the way, my name is Meredith."

Mrs Morgan collapsed on to a hall chair.

"Meredith, miss?" she said incredulously. "Why, I knew your father – "

"I've been married, that's all," said Lydia grimly. "You told me yesterday that I should be married romantically, but even in the wildest flights of your imagination, Mrs Morgan, you could never have supposed that I should be married in such a violent, desperate way. I'm going to bed." She paused on the landing and looked down at the dumbfounded woman. "If anybody calls for me, I am not at home. Oh, yes, you can tell the *Megaphone* that I came home very late and that I've gone to bed, and I'll call tomorrow to explain."

"But, miss," stammered the woman, "your husband – "

"My husband is dead," said the girl calmly. She felt a brute, but somehow she could not raise any note of sorrow. "And if that lawyer man comes, will you please tell him that I shall have twenty thousand pounds in the morning," and with that last staggering statement, she went to her room, leaving her landlady speechless.

6

The police search of the house and grounds at Dulwich Grange, Mr Rennett's residence, occupied the whole of the morning, and neither Rennett's nor Jack's assistance was invited or offered.

Before luncheon Inspector Colhead came to the study.

"We've had a good look round your place, Mr Rennett," he said, "and I think we know where the deceased hid himself."

"Indeed!" said Mr Rennett.

"That hut of yours in the garden is used, I suppose, for a tool house. There are no tools there now, and one of my men discovered that you can pull up the whole of the floor, it works on a hinge and is balanced with counterweights."

Mr Rennett nodded.

"I believe it was used as a wine cellar by a former tenant of the house," he said coolly. "We have no cellars at the Grange, you know. I do not drink wine, and I've never had occasion to use it."

"That's where he was hidden. We found a blanket, and pillows, down there, and, as you say, it has obviously been a wine cellar, because there is a ventilating shaft leading up into the bushes. We should never have found the trap, but one of my men felt one of the corners of the floor give under his feet."

The two men said nothing.

"Another thing," the detective went on slowly, "is that I'm inclined to agree that Meredith did not commit suicide. We found footmarks, quite fresh, leading round to the back of the hut."

"A big foot or a little foot?" asked Jack quickly.

It is rather a big foot," said the detective, "and it has rubber heels. We traced it to a gate at the back of your premises, and the gate has been opened recently – probably by Mr Meredith when he came to the house. It's a queer case, Mr Rennett."

"What is the pistol?"

"That's new too," said Colhead. "Belgian make and impossible to trace, I should imagine. You can't keep track of these Belgian weapons. You can buy them in any shop in any town in Ostend or Brussels, and I don't think it is the practice for the sellers to keep any record of the numbers."

"In fact," said Jack quietly, "it is the same kind of pistol that killed Bulford."

Colhead raised his eyebrows.

"So it was, but wasn't it established that that was Mr Meredith's own weapon?"

Jack shook his head.

"The only thing that was established was that he had seen the body and he picked up the pistol which was lying near the dead man. The shot was fired as he opened the door of Mr Briggerland's house. Then he saw the figure on the pavement and picked up the pistol. He was in that position when Miss Briggerland, who testified against him, came out of the house and saw him."

The detective nodded.

"I had nothing to do with the case," he said, "but I remember seeing the weapon, and it was identical with this. I'll talk to the chief and let you know what he says about the whole affair. You'll have to give evidence at the inquest of course."

When he had gone the two men looked at one another.

"Well, Rennett, do you think we're going to get into hot water, or are we going to perjure our way to safety?"

"There's no need for perjury, not serious perjury," said the other carefully. "By the way, Jack, where was Briggerland the night Bulford was murdered?"

"When Miss Jean Briggerland had recovered from her horror, she went upstairs and aroused her father, who, despite the early hour, was in bed and asleep. When the police came, or rather, when the detective in charge of the case arrived, which must have been some time after the policeman on point duty put in an appearance, Mr Briggerland was discovered in a picturesque dressing gown and, I presume, no less picturesque pyjamas."

"Horrified, too, I suppose," said Rennett dryly. Jack was silent for a long time. Then: "Rennett," he said, "do you know I am more rattled about this girl than I am about any consequences to ourselves."

"Which girl are you talking about?"

"About Mrs Meredith. Whilst poor Meredith was alive she was in no particular danger. But do you realise that what were advantages from our point of view, namely, the fact that she had no relations in the world, are today a source of considerable peril to this unfortunate lady?"

"I had forgotten that," said Rennett thoughtfully. "What makes matters a little more complicated, is the will which Meredith made this morning before he was married."

Jack whistled.

"Did he make a will?" he said in surprise.

His partner nodded.

"You remember he was here with me for half an hour. Well, he insisted upon writing out a will and my wife and Bolton, the butler, witnessed it."

"And he has left his money – ?"

"To his wife absolutely," replied the other.

"The poor old chap was so frantically keen on keeping the money out of the Briggerland exchequer, that he was prepared to entrust the whole of his money to a girl he had not seen."

Jack was serious now.

"And the Briggerlands are her heirs? Do you realise that, Rennett – there's going to be hell!"

Mr Rennett nodded.

"I thought that too," he said quietly.

31

Jack sank down in a seat, his face screwed up into a hideous frown, and the elder man did not interrupt his thoughts. Suddenly Jack's face cleared and he smiled.

"Jaggs!" he said softly.

"Jaggs?" repeated his puzzled partner.

"Jaggs," said Jack, nodding, "he's the fellow. We've got to meet strategy with strategy, Rennett, and Jaggs is the boy to do it."

Mr Rennett looked at him helplessly.

"Could Jaggs get us out of our trouble too?" he asked sarcastically.

"He could even do that," replied Jack.

"Then bring him along, for I have an idea he'll have the time of his life."

7

Miss Jean Briggerland reached her home in Berkeley Street soon after nine o'clock. She did not ring, but let herself in with a key and went straight to the dining-room, where her father sat eating his breakfast, with a newspaper propped up before him.

He was the dark-skinned man whom Lydia had seen at the theatre, and he looked up over his gold-rimmed spectacles as the girl came in.

"You have been out very early," he said.

She did not reply, but slowly divesting herself of her sable coat she threw it on to a chair, took off the toque that graced her shapely head, and flung it after the coat. Then she drew out a chair, and sat down at the table, her chin on her palms, her blue eyes fixed upon her parent.

Nature had so favoured her that her face needed no artificial embellishment – the skin was clear and fine of texture, and the cold morning had brought only a faint pink to the beautiful face.

"Well, my dear," Mr Briggerland looked up and beamed through his glasses, "so poor Meredith has committed suicide?"

She did not speak, keeping her eyes fixed on him.

"Very sad, very sad," Mr Briggerland shook his head.

"How did it happen?" she asked quietly.

Mr Briggerland shrugged his shoulders.

"I suppose at the sight of you he bolted back to his hiding place where – er – had been located by – er – interested persons during the night, then seeing me by the shed – he committed the rash and fatal act. Somehow I thought he would run back to his dugout."

"And you were prepared for him?" she said.

He smiled.

"A clear case of suicide, my dear," he said.

"Shot through the left temple, and the pistol was found in his right hand," said the girl.

Mr Briggerland started.

"Damn it," he said. "Who noticed that?"

"That good-looking young lawyer, Glover."

"Did the police notice?"

"I suppose they did when Glover called their attention to the fact," said the girl.

Mr Briggerland took off his glasses and wiped them.

"It was done in such a hurry – I had to get back through the garden gate to join the police. When I got there, I found they'd been attracted by the shot and had entered the house. Still, nobody would know I was in the garden, and anyway my association with the capture of an escaped convict would not get into the newspapers."

"But a case of suicide would," said the girl. "Though I don't suppose the police will give away the person who informed them that James Meredith would be at Dulwich Grange."

Mr Briggerland sat back in his chair, his thick lips pursed, and he was not a beautiful sight.

"One can't remember everything," he grumbled.

He rose from his chair, went to the door, and locked it. Then he crossed to a bureau, pulled open a drawer and took out a small revolver. He threw out the cylinder, glanced along the barrel and the chambers to make sure it was not loaded, then clicked it back in position, and standing before a glass, he endeavoured, the pistol in his right hand, to bring the muzzle to bear on his left temple. He found this impossible, and signified his annoyance with a grunt. Then he tried the pistol with his thumb on the trigger and his hand clasping the back of the butt. Here he was more successful.

"That's it," he said with satisfaction. "It could have been done that way."

She did not shudder at the dreadful sight, but watched him with the keenest interest, her chin still in the palm of her hand. He might have been explaining a new way of serving a tennis ball, for all the emotion he evoked.

Mr Briggerland came back to the table, toyed with a piece of toast and buttered it leisurely.

"Everybody is going to Cannes this year," he said, "but I think I shall stick to Monte Carlo. There is a quiet about Monte Carlo which is very restful, especially if one can get a villa on the hill away from the railway. I told Morden yesterday to take the new car across and meet us at Boulogne. He says that the new body is exquisite. There is a microphonic attachment for telephoning to the driver, the electrical heating apparatus is splendid and – "

"Meredith was married."

If she had thrown a bomb at him she could not have produced a more tremendous sensation. He gaped at her, and pushed himself back from the table.

"Married?" His voice was a squeak.

She nodded.

"It's a lie," he roared. All his suavity dropped away from him, his face was distorted and puckered with anger and grew a shade darker. "Married, you lying little beast! He couldn't have been married! It was only a few minutes after eight, and the parson didn't come till nine. I'll break your neck if you try to scare me! I've told you about that before…"

He raved on, and she listened unmoved.

"He was married at eight o'clock by a man they brought down from Oxford, and who stayed the night in the house," she repeated with great calmness. "There's no sense in lashing yourself into a rage. I've seen the bride, and spoken to the clergyman."

From the bullying, raging madman, he became a whimpering, pitiable thing. His chin trembled, the big hands he laid on the tablecloth shook with a fever.

"What are we going to do?" he wailed. "My God, Jean, what are we going to do?"

She rose and went to the sideboard, poured out a stiff dose of brandy from a decanter and brought it across to him without a word.

She was used to these tantrums, and to their inevitable ending. She was neither hurt, surprised, nor disgusted. This pale, ethereal being was the dominant partner of the combination. Nerves she did not possess, fears she did not know. She had acquired the precise sense of a great surgeon in whom pity was a detached emotion, and one which never intruded itself into the operating chamber. She was no more phenomenal than they, save that she did not feel bound by the conventions and laws which govern them as members of an ordered society. It requires no greater nerve to slay than to cure. She had had that matter out with herself, and had settled it to her own satisfaction.

"You will have to put off your trip to Monte Carlo," she said, as he drank the brandy greedily.

"We've lost everything now," he stuttered, "everything."

"This girl has no relations," said the daughter steadily. "Her heirs-at-law are ourselves."

He put down the glass, and looked at her, and became almost immediately his old self.

"My dear," he said admiringly, "you are really wonderful. Of course, it was childish of me. Now what do you suggest?"

"Unlock that door," she said in a low voice, "I want to call the maid."

As he walked to the door, she pressed the footbell, and soon after the faded woman who attended her came into the room.

"Hart," she said, "I want you to find my emerald ring, the small one, the little pearl necklet, and the diamond scarf pin. Pack them carefully in a box with cotton wool."

"Yes, madam," said the woman, and went out.

"Now what are you going to do, Jean?" asked her father.

"I am returning them to Mrs Meredith," said the girl coolly. "They were presents given to me by her husband, and I feel after this tragic ending of my dream that I can no longer bear the sight of them."

"He didn't give you those things, he gave you the chain. Besides, you are throwing away good money?"

"I know he never gave them to me, and I am not throwing away good money," she said patiently. "Mrs Meredith will return them, and she will give me an opportunity of throwing a little light upon James Meredith, an opportunity which I very much desire."

Later she went up to her pretty little sitting-room on the first floor, and wrote a letter.

DEAR MRS MEREDITH,

I am sending you the few trinkets which James gave to me in happier days. They are all that I have of his, and you, as a woman, will realise that whilst the possession of them brings me many unhappy memories, yet they have been a certain comfort to me. I wish I could dispose of memory as easily as I send these to you (for I feel they are really your property) but more do I wish that I could recall and obliterate the occasion which has made Mr Glover so bitter an enemy of mine.

Thinking over the past, I see that I was at fault, but I know that you will sympathise with me when the truth is revealed to you. A young girl, unused to the ways of men, perhaps I attached too much importance to Mr Glover's attentions, and resented them too crudely. In those days I thought it was unpardonable that a man who professed to be poor James's best friend, should make love to his fiancée, though I suppose that such things happen, and are endured by the modern girl. A man does not readily forgive a woman for making him feel a fool – it is the one unpardonable offence that a girl can commit. Therefore, I do not resent his enmity as much as you might think. Believe me, I feel for you very much in these trying days. Let me say again that I hope your future will be bright.

She blotted the letter, put it in an envelope, and addressed it, and taking down a book from one of the well-stocked shelves, drew her chair to the fire, and began reading.

Mr Briggerland came in an hour after, looked over her shoulder at the title, and made a sound of disapproval.

"I can't understand your liking for that kind of book," he said.

The book was one of the two volumes of "Chronicles of Crime", and she looked up with a smile.

"Can't you? It's very easily explained. It is the most encouraging work in my collection. Sit down for a minute."

"A record of vulgar criminals," he growled. "Their infernal last dying speeches, their processions to Tyburn – phaugh!"

She smiled again, and looked down at the book. The wide margins were covered with pencilled notes in her writing.

"They're a splendid mental exercise," she said. "In every case I have written down how the criminal might have escaped arrest, but they were all so vulgar, and so stupid. Really the police of the time deserve no credit for catching them. It is the same with modern criminals…"

She went to the shelf, and took down two large scrapbooks, carried them across to the fire, and opened one on her knees.

"Vulgar and stupid, every one of them," she repeated, as she turned the leaves rapidly.

"The clever ones get caught at times," said Briggerland gloomily.

"Never," she said, and closed the book with a snap. "In England, in France, in America, and in almost every civilised country, there are murderers walking about today, respected by their fellow citizens. Murderers, of whose crimes the police are ignorant. Look at these." She opened the book again. "Here is the case of Rell, who poisons a troublesome creditor with weedkiller. Everybody in the town knew he bought the weedkiller; everybody knew that he was in debt to this man. What chance had he of escaping? Here's Jewelville – he kills his wife, buries her in the cellar, and then calls attention to himself by running away. Here's Morden, who kills his sister-in-law for the sake of her insurance money, and who also buys the poison in broad daylight, and is found with a bottle in his pocket. Such people deserve hanging."

"I wish to heaven you wouldn't talk about hanging," said Briggerland tremulously, "you're inhuman, Jean, by God – "

"I'm an angel," she smiled, "and I have press cuttings to prove it! The *Daily Recorder* had half a column on my appearance in the box at Jim's trial."

He looked over toward the writing table, saw the letter, and picked it up.

"So you've written to the lady. Are you sending her the jewels?"

She nodded.

He looked at her quickly.

"You haven't been up to any funny business with them, have you?" he asked suspiciously, and she smiled.

"My dear parent," drawled Jean Briggerland, "after my lecture on the stupidity of the average criminal, do you imagine I should do anything so *gauche*?"

8

"And now, Mrs Meredith," said Jack Glover, "what are you going to do?"

He had spent the greater part of the morning with the new heiress, and Lydia had listened, speechless, as he recited a long and meaningless list of securities, of estates, of ground rents, balances and the like, which she had inherited.

"What am I going to do?" she said, shaking her head, hopelessly. "I don't know. I haven't the slightest idea, Mr Glover. It is so bewildering. Do I understand that all this property is mine?"

"Not yet," said Jack with a smile, "but it is so much yours that on the strength of the will we are willing to advance you money to almost any extent. The will has to be proved, and probate must be taken, but when these legal formalities are settled, and we have paid the very heavy death duties, you will be entitled to dispose of your fortune as you wish. As a matter of fact," he added, "you could do that now. At any rate, you cannot live here in Brinksome Street, and I have taken the liberty of hiring a furnished flat on your behalf. One of our clients has gone away to the Continent and left the flat for me to dispose of. The rent is very low, about twenty guineas a week."

"Twenty guineas a week!" gasped the horrified girl, "why, I can't – "

And then she realised that she "could".

Twenty guineas a week was as nothing to her. This fact more than anything else, brought her to an understanding of her fortune.

"I suppose I had better move," she said dubiously. "Mrs Morgan is giving up this house, and she asked me whether I had any plans. I think she'd be willing to come as my housekeeper."

"Excellent," nodded Jack. "You'll want a maid as well and, of course, you will have to put up Jaggs for the nights."

"Jaggs?" she said in astonishment.

"Jaggs," repeated Jack solemnly. "You see, Miss – I beg your pardon, Mrs Meredith, I'm rather concerned about you, and I want you to have somebody on hand I can rely on, sleeping in your flat at night. I dare say you think I am an old woman," he said as he saw her smile, "and that my fears are groundless, but you will agree that your own experience of last week will support the theory that anything may happen in London."

"But really, Mr Glover, you don't mean that I am in any serious danger – from whom?"

"From a lot of people," he said diplomatically.

"From poor Miss Briggerland?" she challenged, and his eyes narrowed.

"Poor Miss Briggerland," he said softly. "She certainly is poorer than she expected to be."

"Nonsense," scoffed the girl. She was irritated, which was unusual in her. "My dear Mr Glover, why do you pursue your vendetta against her? Do you think it is playing the game, honestly now? Isn't it a case of wounded vanity on your part?"

He stared at her in astonishment.

"Wounded vanity? Do you mean pique?"

She nodded.

"Why should I be piqued?" he asked slowly.

"You know best," replied Lydia, and then a light dawned on him.

"Have I been making love to Miss Briggerland by any chance?" he asked.

"You know best," she repeated.

"Good Lord!" and then he began to laugh, and she thought he would never stop.

41

"I suppose I made love to her, and she was angry because I dared to commit such an act of treachery to her fiancé! Yes, that was it. I made love to her behind poor Jim's back, and she 'ticked me off', and that's why I'm so annoyed with her?"

"You have a very good memory," said Lydia, with a scornful little smile.

"My memory isn't as good as Miss Briggerland's power of invention," said Jack. "Doesn't it strike you, Mrs Meredith, that if I had made love to that young lady, I should not be seen here today?"

"What do you mean?" she asked.

"I mean," said Jack Glover soberly, "that it would not have been Bulford, but I, who would have been lured from his club by a telephone message, and told to wait outside the door in Berkeley Street. It would have been I, who would have been shot dead by Miss Briggerland's father from the drawing-room window."

The girl looked at him in amazement.

"What a preposterous charge to make!" she said at last indignantly. "Do you suggest that this girl has connived at a murder?"

"I not only suggest that she connived at it, but I stake my life that she planned it," said Jack carefully.

"But the pistol was found near Mr Bulford's body," said Lydia almost triumphantly, as she conceived this unanswerable argument.

Jack nodded.

"From Bulford's body to the drawing-room window was exactly nine feet. It was possible to pitch the pistol so that it fell near him. Bulford was waiting there by the instructions of Jean Briggerland. We have traced the telephone call that came through to him from the club – it came from the Briggerlands' house in Berkeley Street, and the attendant at the club was sure it was a woman's voice. We didn't find that out till after the trial. Poor Meredith was in the hall when the shot was fired. The signal was given when he turned the handle to let himself out. He heard the shot, rushed down the steps and saw the body. Whether he picked up the pistol or not, I do not know. Jean Briggerland swears he had it in his hand, but, of course, Jean Briggerland is a hopeless liar!"

"You can't know what you're saying," said Lydia in a low voice. "It is a dreadful charge to make, dreadful, against a girl whose very face refutes such an accusation."

"Her face is her fortune," snapped Jack, and then penitently, "I'm sorry I'm rude, but somehow the very mention of Jean Briggerland arouses all that is worst in me. Now, you will accept Jaggs, won't you?"

"Who is he?" she asked.

"He is an old army pensioner. A weird bird, as shrewd as the dickens, in spite of his age a pretty powerful old fellow."

"Oh, he's old," she said with some relief.

"He's old, and in some ways, incapacitated. He hasn't the use of his right arm, and he's a bit groggy in one of his ankles as the result of a Boer bullet."

She laughed in spite of herself.

"He doesn't sound a very attractive kind of guardian. He's a perfectly clean old bird, though I confess he doesn't look it, and he won't bother you or your servants. You can give him a room where he can sit, and you can give him a bit of bread and cheese, and a glass of beer, and he'll not bother you."

Lydia was amused now. It was absurd that Jack Glover should imagine she needed a guardian at all, but if he insisted, as he did, it would be better to have somebody as harmless as the unattractive Jaggs.

"What time will he come?"

"At about ten o'clock every night, and he'll leave you at about seven in the morning. Unless you wish, you need never see him," said Jack.

"How did you come to know him?" she asked curiously.

"I know everybody," said the boastful young man, "you mustn't forget that I am a lawyer and have to meet very queer people."

He gathered up his papers and put them into his little bag.

"And now what are your plans for today?" he demanded.

She resented the self-imposed guardianship which he had undertaken, yet she could not forget what she owed him.

By some extraordinary means he had kept her out of the Meredith case and she had not been called as a witness at the inquest. Incidentally, in as mysterious a way he had managed to whitewash his partner and himself, although the Law Society were holding an inquiry of their own (this the girl did not know) and it seemed likely that he would escape the consequence of an act which was a flagrant breach of the law.

"I am going to Mrs Cole-Mortimer's to tea," she said.

"Mrs Cole-Mortimer?" he said quickly. "How do you come to know that lady?"

"Really, Mr Glover, you are almost impertinent," she smiled in spite of her annoyance. "She came to call on me two or three days after that dreadful morning. She knew Mr Meredith and was an old friend of the family's."

"As a matter of fact," said Jack icily, "she did not know Meredith, except to say 'how-do-you-do' to him, and she was certainly not a friend of the family. She is, however, a friend of Jean Briggerland."

"Jean Briggerland!" said the exasperated girl. "Can't you forget her? You are like the man in Dickens' books – she's your King Charles' head! Really, for a respectable and a responsible lawyer, you're simply eaten up with prejudices. Of course, she was a friend of Mr Meredith's. Why, she brought me a photograph of him taken when he was at Eton."

"Supplied by Jean Briggerland," said the unperturbed Jack calmly, "and if she'd brought you a pair of socks he wore when he was a baby I suppose you would have accepted those too."

"Now you are being really abominable," said the girl, "and I've got a lot to do."

He paused at the door.

"Don't forget you can move into Cavendish Mansions tomorrow. I'll send the key round, and the day you move in, Jaggs will turn up for duty, bright and smiling. He doesn't talk a great deal – "

"I don't suppose you ever give the poor man a chance," she said cuttingly.

9

Mrs Cole-Mortimer was a representative of a numerous class of women who live so close to the borderline which separates good society from society which is not quite as good, that the members of either set thought she was in the other. She had a small house where she gave big parties, and nobody quite knew how this widow of an Indian colonel made both ends meet. It was the fact that her ménage was an expensive one to maintain; she had a car, she entertained in London in the season, and disappeared from the metropolis when it was the correct thing to disappear, a season of exile which comes between the Goodwood Race Meeting in the south and the Doncaster Race Meeting in the north.

Lydia had been surprised to receive a visit from this elegant lady, and had readily accepted the story of her friendship with James Meredith. Mrs Cole-Mortimer's invitation she had welcomed. She needed some distraction, something which would smooth out the ravelled threads of life which were now even more tangled than she had ever expected they could be.

Mr Rennett had handed to her a thousand pounds the day after the wedding, and when she had recovered from the shock of possessing such a large sum, she hired a taxicab and indulged herself in a wild orgy of shopping.

The relief she experienced when he informed her he was taking charge of her affairs and settling the debts which had worried her for three years was so great that she felt as though a heavy weight had been lifted from her heart.

It was in one of her new frocks that Lydia, feeling more confident than usual, made her call. She had expected to find a crowd at the house in Hyde Park Crescent, and she was surprised when she was ushered into the drawing-room to find only four people present.

Mrs Cole-Mortimer was a chirpy, pale little woman of forty-something. It would be ungallant to say how much that "something" represented. She came toward Lydia with outstretched hands.

"My dear," she said with extravagant pleasure, "I am glad you were able to come. You know Miss Briggerland and Mr Briggerland?"

Lydia looked up at the tall figure of the man she had seen in the stalls the night before her wedding and recognised him instantly.

"Mr Marcus Stepney, I don't think you have met."

Lydia bowed at a smart-looking man of thirty, immaculately attired. He was very handsome, she thought, in a dark way, but he was just a little too "new" to please her. She did not like fashion-plate men, and although the most captious of critics could not have found fault with his correct attire, he gave her the impression of being overdressed.

Lydia had not expected to meet Miss Briggerland and her father, although she had a dim recollection that Mrs Cole-Mortimer had mentioned her name. Then in a flash she recalled the suspicions of Jack Glover, which she had covered with ridicule. The association made her feel a little uncomfortable, and Jean Briggerland, whose intuition was a little short of uncanny, must have read the doubt in her face.

"Mrs Meredith expected to see us, didn't she, Margaret?" she said, addressing the twittering hostess. "Surely you told her we were great friends?"

"Of course I did, my dear. Knowing your dear cousin and his dear father, it was not remarkable that I should know the whole of the family," and she smiled wisely from one to the other.

Of course! How absurd she was, thought Lydia. She had almost forgotten, and probably Jack Glover had forgotten too, that the Briggerlands and the Merediths were related.

She found herself talking in a corner of the room with the girl, and fell to studying her face anew. A closer inspection merely consolidated her earlier judgment. She smiled inwardly as she remembered Jack Glover's ridiculous warning. It was like killing a butterfly with a steam hammer, to loose so much vengeance against this frail piece of china.

"And how do you feel now that you're very rich?" asked Jean kindly.

"I haven't realised it yet," smiled Lydia.

Jean nodded.

"I suppose you have yet to settle with the lawyers. Who are they? Oh yes, of course Mr Glover was poor Jim's solicitor." She sighed. "I dislike lawyers," she said with a shiver, "they are so heavily paternal! They feel that they and they only are qualified to direct your life and your actions. I suppose it is second nature with them. Then, of course, they make an awful lot of money out of commissions and fees, though I'm sure Jack Glover wouldn't worry about that. He's really a nice boy," she said earnestly, "and I don't think you could have a better friend."

Lydia glowed at the generosity of this girl whom the man had so maligned.

"He has been very good to me," she said, "although, of course, he is a little fussy."

Jean's lips twitched with amusement.

"Has he warned you against me?" she asked solemnly. "Has he told you what a terrible ogre I am?" And then without waiting for a reply: "I sometimes think poor Jack is just a little – well, I wouldn't say mad, but a little queer. His dislikes are so violent. He positively loathes Margaret, though why I have never been able to understand."

"He doesn't hate me," laughed Lydia, and Jean looked at her strangely.

"No, I suppose not," she said. "I can't imagine anybody hating you, Lydia. May I call you by your Christian name?"

"I wish you would," said Lydia warmly.

"I can't imagine anybody hating you," repeated the girl thoughtfully. "And, of course, Jack wouldn't hate you because you're

47

his client – a very rich and attractive client too, my dear." She tapped the girl's cheek and Lydia, for some reason, felt foolish.

But as though unconscious of the embarrassment she had caused, Jean went on.

"I don't really blame him, either. I've a shrewd suspicion that all these warnings against me and against other possible enemies will furnish a very excellent excuse for seeing you every day and acting as your personal bodyguard!"

Lydia shook her head.

"That part of it he has relegated already," she said, giving smile for smile. "He has appointed Mr Jaggs as my bodyguard."

"Mr Jaggs?" The tone was even, the note of inquiry was not strained.

"He's an old gentleman in whom Mr Glover is interested, an old army pensioner. Beyond the fact that he hasn't the use of his right arm, and limps with his left leg, and that he likes beer and cheese, he seems an admirable watchdog," said Lydia humorously.

"Jaggs?" repeated the girl. "I wonder where I've heard that name before. Is he a detective?"

"No, I don't think so. But Mr Glover thinks I ought to have some sort of man sleeping in my new flat and Jaggs was duly engaged."

Soon after this Mr Marcus Stepney came over and Lydia found him rather uninteresting. Less boring was Briggerland, for he had a fund of stories and experiences to relate, and he had, too, one of those soft soothing voices that are so rare in men.

It was dark when she came out with Mr and Miss Briggerland, and she felt that the afternoon had not been unprofitably spent.

For she had a clearer conception of the girl's character, and was getting Jack Glover's interest into better perspective. The mercenary part of it made her just a little sick. There was something so mysterious, so ugly in his outlook on life, and there might not be a little self-interest in his care for her.

She stood on the step of the house talking to the girl, whilst Mr Briggerland lit a cigarette with a patent lighter. Hyde Park Crescent was deserted save for a man who stood near the railings which protected the area of Mrs Cole-Mortimer's house. He was apparently tying his shoelaces.

They went down on the sidewalk, and Mr Briggerland looked for his car.

"I'd like to take you home. My chauffeur promised to be here at four o'clock. These men are most untrustworthy."

From the other end of the Crescent appeared the lights of a car. At first Lydia thought it might be Mr Briggerland's, and she was going to make her excuses for she wanted to go home alone. The car was coming too, at a tremendous pace. She watched it as it came furiously toward her, and she did not notice that Mr Briggerland and his daughter had left her standing alone on the sidewalk and had withdrawn a few paces.

Suddenly the car made a swerve, mounted the sidewalk and dashed upon her. It seemed that nothing could save her, and she stood fascinated with horror, waiting for death.

Then an arm gripped her waist, a powerful arm that lifted her from her feet and flung her back against the railings, as the car flashed past, the mudguard missing her by an inch. The machine pulled up with a jerk, and the white-faced girl saw Briggerland and Jean running toward her.

"I should never have forgiven myself if anything had happened. I think my chauffeur must be drunk," said Briggerland in an agitated voice.

She had no words. She could only nod, and then she remembered her preserver, and she turned to meet the solemn eyes of a bent old man, whose pointed, white beard and bristling white eyebrows gave him a hawklike appearance. His right hand was thrust into his pocket. He was touching his battered hat with the other.

"Beg pardon, miss," he said raucously, "name of Jaggs! And I have reported for dooty!"

10

Jack Glover listened gravely to the story which the girl told. He had called at her lodgings on the following morning to secure her signature to some documents, and breathlessly and a little shamefacedly, she told him what had happened.

"Of course it was an accident," she insisted, "in fact, Mr and Miss Briggerland were almost knocked down by the car. But you don't know how thankful I am your Mr Jaggs was on the spot."

"Where is he now?" asked Jack.

"I don't know," replied the girl. "He just limped away without another word and I did not see him again, though I thought I caught a glimpse of him as I came into this house last night. How did he come to be on the spot?" she asked curiously.

"That is easily explained," replied Jack. "I told the old boy not to let you out of his sight from sundown to sunup."

"Then you think I'm safe during the day?" she rallied him.

He nodded.

"I don't know whether to laugh at you or to be very angry," she said, shaking her head reprovingly. "Of course it was an accident!"

"I disagree with you," said Jack. "Did you catch a glimpse of the chauffeur?"

"No," she said in surprise. "I didn't think of looking at him."

He nodded.

"If you had, you would probably have seen an old friend, namely, the gentleman who carried you off from the Erving Theatre," he said quietly.

It was difficult for Lydia to analyse her own feelings. She knew that Jack Glover was wrong, monstrously wrong. She was perfectly confident that his fantastic theory had no foundation, and yet she could not get away from his sincerity. Remembering Jean's description of him as "a little queer" she tried to fit that description into her knowledge of him, only to admit to herself that he had been exceptionally normal as far as she was concerned. The suggestion that his object was mercenary, and that he looked upon her as a profitable match for himself, she dismissed without consideration.

"Anyway, I like your Mr Jaggs," she said.

"Better than you like me, I gather from your tone," smiled Jack. "He's not a bad old boy."

"He is a very strong old boy," she said. "He lifted me as though I were a feather – I don't know now how I escaped. The steering gear went wrong," she explained unnecessarily.

"Dear me," said Jack politely, "and it went right again in time to enable the chauffeur to keep clear of Briggerland and his angel daughter!"

She gave a gesture of despair.

"You're hopeless," she said. "These things happened in the dark ages; men and women do not assassinate one another in the twentieth century."

"Who told you that?" he demanded. "Human nature hasn't changed for two thousand years. The instinct to kill is as strong as ever, or wars would be impossible. If any man or woman could commit one cold-blooded murder, there is no reason why he or she should not commit a hundred. In England, America, and France fifty cold-blooded murders are detected every year. Twice that number are undetected. It does not make the crime more impossible because the criminal is good-looking."

"You're hopeless," she said again, and Jack made no further attempt to convince her.

On the Thursday of that week she exchanged her lodgings for a handsome flat in Cavendish Place, and Mrs Morgan had promised to join her a week later, when she had settled up her own business affairs.

Lydia was fortunate enough to get two maids from one of the agencies, one of whom was to sleep on the premises. The flat was not illimitable, and she regretted that she had promised to place a room at the disposal of the aged Mr Jaggs. If he was awake all night as she presumed he would be, and slept in the day, he might have been accommodated in the kitchen, and she hinted as much to Jack. To her surprise the lawyer had turned down that idea.

"You don't want your servants to know that you have a watchman."

"What do you imagine they will think he is?" she asked scornfully. "How can I have an old gentleman in the flat without explaining why he is there?"

"Your explanation could be that he did the boots."

"It wouldn't take him all night to do the boots. Of course, I'm too grateful to him to want him to do anything."

Mr Jaggs reported again for duty that night. He came at half past nine, a shabby-looking old man, and Lydia, who had not yet got used to her new magnificence, came out into the hall to meet him.

He was certainly not a prepossessing object, and Lydia discovered that, in addition to his other misfortunes, he had a slight squint.

"I hadn't an opportunity of thanking you the other day, Mr Jaggs," she said. "I think you saved my life."

"That's all right, miss," he said, in his hoarse voice. "Dooty is dooty!"

She thought he was looking past her, till she realised that his curious slanting line of vision was part of his infirmity.

"I'll show you to your room," she said hastily.

She led the way down the corridor, opened the door of a small room which had been prepared for him, and switched on the light.

"Too much light for me, miss," said the old man, shaking his head. "I like to sit in the dark and listen, that's what I like, to sit in the dark and listen."

"But you can't sit in the dark, you'll want to read, won't you?"

"Can't read, miss," said Jaggs cheerfully. "Can't write, either. I don't know that I'm any worse off."

Reluctantly she switched out the light.

"But you won't be able to see your food."

"I can feel for that, miss," he said with a hoarse chuckle. "Don't you worry about me. I'll just sit here and have a big think."

If she was uncomfortable before, she was really embarrassed now. The very sight of the door behind which old Jaggs sat having his "big think" was an irritation to her. She could not sleep for a long time that night for thinking of him sitting in the darkness, and "listening" as he put it, and had firmly resolved on ending a condition of affairs which was particularly distasteful to her, when she fell asleep.

She woke when the maid brought her tea, to learn that Jaggs had gone.

The maid, too, had her views on the "old gentleman". She hadn't slept all night for the thought of him, she said, though probably this was an exaggeration.

The arrangement must end, thought Lydia, and she called at Jack Glover's office that afternoon to tell him so. Jack listened without comment until she had finished.

"I'm sorry he is worrying you, but you'll get used to him in time, and I should be obliged if you kept him for a month. You would relieve me of a lot of anxiety."

At first she was determined to have her way, but he was so persistent, so pleading, that eventually she surrendered.

Lucy, the new maid, however, was not so easily convinced.

"I don't like it, miss," she said, "he's just like an old tramp, and I'm sure we shall be murdered in our beds."

"How cheerful you are, Lucy," laughed Lydia. "Of course, there is no danger from Mr Jaggs, and he really was very useful to me."

The girl grumbled and assented a little sulkily, and Lydia had a feeling that she was going to lose a good servant. In this she was not mistaken.

Old Jaggs called at half past nine that night, and was admitted by the maid, who stalked in front of him and opened his door.

"There's your room," she snapped, "and I'd rather have your room than your company."

"Would you, miss?" wheezed Jaggs, and Lydia, attracted by the sound of voices, came to the door and listened with some amusement.

"Lord, bless me life, it ain't a bad room, either. Put the light out, my dear, I don't like light. I like 'em dark, like them little cells in Holloway prison, where you were took two years ago for robbing your missus."

Lydia's smile left her face. She heard the girl gasp.

"You old liar!" she hissed.

"Lucy Jones you call yourself – you used to be Mary Welch in them days," chuckled old Jaggs.

"I'm not going to be insulted," almost screamed Lucy, though there was a note of fear in her strident voice. "I'm going to leave tonight."

"No you ain't, my dear," said old Jaggs complacently. "You're going to sleep here tonight, and you're going to leave in the morning. If you try to get out of that door before I let you, you'll be pinched."

"They've got nothing against me," the girl was betrayed into saying.

"False characters, my dear. Pretending to come from the agency, when you didn't. That's another crime. Lord bless your heart, I've got enough against you to put you in jail for a year."

Lydia came forward.

"What is this you're saying about my maid?"

"Good evening, ma'am."

The old man knuckled his forehead.

"I'm just having an argument with your young lady."

"Do you say she is a thief?"

"Of course she is, miss," said Jaggs scornfully. "You ask her!"

But Lucy had gone into her room, slammed the door and locked it.

The next morning when Lydia woke, the flat was empty, save for herself. But she had hardly finished dressing when there came a knock at the door, and a trim, fresh-looking country girl, with an expansive smile and a look of good cheer that warmed Lydia's heart, appeared.

"You're the lady that wants a maid, ma'am, aren't you?"

"Yes," said Lydia in surprise. "But who sent you?"

"I was telegraphed for yesterday, ma'am, from the country."

"Come in," said Lydia helplessly.

"Isn't it right?" asked the girl a little disappointedly. "They sent me my fare. I came up by the first train."

"It is quite all right," said Lydia, "only I'm wondering who is running this flat, me or Mr Jaggs?"

11

Jean Briggerland had spent a very busy afternoon. There had been a string of callers at the handsome house in Berkeley Street.

Mr Briggerland was of a philanthropic bent, and had instituted a club in the East End of London which was intended to raise the moral tone of Limehouse, Wapping, Poplar and the adjacent districts. It was started without ostentation, with a man named Faire as general manager. Mr Faire had had in his lifetime several hectic contests with the police, in which he had been invariably the loser. And it was in his role as a reformed character that he undertook the management of this social uplift club.

Well-meaning police officials had warned Mr Briggerland that Faire had a bad character. Mr Briggerland listened, was grateful for the warning, but explained that Faire had come under the influence of the new uplift movement and from henceforward he would be an exemplary citizen. Later, the police had occasion to extend their warning to its founder. The club was being used by known criminal characters; men who had already been in jail and were qualifying for a return visit.

Again Mr Briggerland pointed to the object of the institution which was to bring bad men into the society of good men and women, and to arouse in them a desire for better things. He quoted a famous text with great effect. But still the police were unconvinced.

It was the practice of Miss Jean Briggerland to receive selected members of the club and to entertain them at tea in Berkeley Street. Her friends thought it was very "sweet" and very "daring", and wondered whether she wasn't afraid of catching some kind of disease peculiar to the East End of London. But Jean did not worry about such things. On this afternoon, after the last of her callers had gone, she went down to the little morning room where such entertainments occurred and found two men, who rose awkwardly as she entered.

The gentle influence of the club had not made them look anything but what they were. "Jailbird" was written all over them.

"I'm very glad you men have come," said Jean sweetly. "Mr Hoggins – "

"That's me, miss," said one, with a grin.

"And Mr Talmot."

The second man showed his teeth.

"I'm always glad to see members of the club," said Jean busy with the teapot, "especially men who have had so bad a time as you have. You have only just come out of prison, haven't you, Mr Hoggins?" she asked innocently.

Hoggins went red and coughed.

"Yes, miss," he said huskily and added inconsequently, "I didn't do it!"

"I'm sure you were innocent," she said with a smile of sympathy, "and really if you were guilty I don't think you men are so much to blame. Look what a bad time you have! What disadvantages you suffer, whilst here in the West End people are wasting money that really ought to go to your wives and children."

"That's right," said Mr Hoggins.

"There's a girl I know who is tremendously rich," Jean prattled on. "She lives at 84, Cavendish Mansions, just on the top floor, and, of course, she's very foolish to sleep with her windows open, especially as people could get down from the roof – there is a fire escape there. She always has a lot of jewellery – keeps it under her pillow I think, and there is generally a few hundred pounds scattered about the bedroom. Now that is what I call putting temptation in the way of the weak."

She lifted her blue eyes, saw the glitter in the man's eyes and went on.

"I've told her lots of times that there is danger, but she only laughs. There is an old man who sleeps in the house – quite a feeble old man who has only the use of one arm. Of course, if she cried out, I suppose he would come to her rescue, but then a real burglar wouldn't let her cry out, would he?" she asked.

The two men looked at one another.

"No," breathed one.

"Especially as they could get clean away if they were clever," said Jean, "and it isn't likely that they would leave her in a condition to betray them, is it?"

Mr Hoggins cleared his throat.

"It's not very likely, miss," he said.

Jean shrugged her shoulders.

"Women do these things, and then they blame the poor man to whom a thousand pounds would be a fortune because he comes and takes it. Personally, I should not like to live at 84, Cavendish Mansions."

"84, Cavendish Mansions," murmured Mr Hoggins absent-mindedly.

His last sentence had been one of ten years' penal servitude. His next sentence would be for life. Nobody knew this better than Jean Briggerland as she went on to talk of the club and of the wonderful work which it was doing.

She dismissed her visitors and went back to her sitting-room. As she turned to go up the stairway her maid intercepted her.

"Mary is in your room, miss," she said in a low voice.

Jean frowned but made no reply.

The woman who stood awkwardly in the centre of the room awaiting the girl, greeted her with an apologetic smile.

"I'm sorry, miss," she said, "but I lost my job this morning. That old man spotted me. He's a split – a detective."

Jean Briggerland regarded her with an unmoved face save that her beautiful mouth took on the pathetic little droop which had excited the pity of a judge and an army of lawyers.

"When did this happen?" she asked. "Last night, miss. He came and I got a bit cheeky to him, and he turned on me, the old devil, and told me my real name and that I'd got the job by forging recommendations."

Jean sat down slowly in the padded Venetian chair before her writing table.

"Jaggs?" she asked.

"Yes, miss."

"And why didn't you come here at once?"

"I thought I might be followed, miss."

The girl bit her lip and nodded.

"You did quite right," she said, and then after a moment's reflection, "We shall be in Paris next week. You had better go by the night train and wait for us at the flat."

She gave the maid some money and after she had gone, sat for an hour before the fire looking into its red depths.

She rose at last a little stiffly, pulled the heavy silken curtain across the windows and switched on the light, and there was a smile on her face that was very beautiful to see. For in that hour came an inspiration.

She sought her father in his study and told him her plan, and he blanched and shivered with the very horror of it.

12

Mr Briggerland, it seemed, had some other object in life than the regeneration of the criminal classes. He was a sociologist – a loose title which covers a great deal of inquisitive investigation into other people's affairs. Moreover, he had published a book on the subject. His name was on the title page and the book had been reviewed to his credit; though in truth he did no more than suggest the title, the work in question having been carried out by a writer on the subject who, for a consideration, had allowed Mr Briggerland to adopt the child of his brain.

On a morning when pale yellow sunlight brightened his dining-room, Mr Briggerland put down his newspaper and looked across the table at his daughter. He had a club in the East End of London and his manager had telephoned that morning sending a somewhat unhappy report.

"Do you remember that man Talmot, my dear?" he asked.

She nodded, and looked up quickly.

"Yes, what about him?"

"He's in hospital," said Mr Briggerland. "I fear that he and Hoggins were engaged in some nefarious plan and that in making an attempt to enter – as, of course, they had no right to enter – a block of flats in Cavendish Place, poor Talmot slipped and fell from the fourth floor window sill, breaking his leg. Hoggins had to carry him to hospital."

The girl reached for bacon from the hot plate.

"He should have broken his neck," she said calmly. "I suppose now the police are making tender inquiries?"

"No, no," Mr Briggerland hastened to assure her. "Nobody knows anything about it, not even the – er – fortunate occupant of the flat they were evidently trying to burgle. I only learnt of it because the manager of the club, who gets information of this character, thought I would be interested."

"Anyway I'm glad they didn't succeed," said Jean after a while. "The possibility of their trying rather worried me. The Hoggins type is such a bungler that it was almost certain they would fail."

It was a curious fact that whilst her father made the most guarded references to all their exploits and clothed them with garments of euphemism, his daughter never attempted any such disguise. The psychologist would find in Mr Briggerland's reticence the embryo of a once dominant rectitude, no trace of which remained in his daughter's moral equipment.

"I have been trying to place this man Jaggs," she went on with a little puzzled frown, "and he completely baffles me. He arrives every night in a taxicab, sometimes from St Pancras, sometimes from Euston, sometimes from London Bridge Station."

"Do you think he is a detective?"

"I don't know," she said thoughtfully. "If he is, he has been imported from the provinces. He is not a Scotland Yard man. He may, of course, be an old police pensioner, and I have been trying to trace him from that source."

"It should not be difficult to find out all about him," said Mr Briggerland easily. "A man with his afflictions should be pretty well known."

He looked at his watch.

"My appointment at Norwood is at eleven o'clock," he said. He made a little grimace of disgust.

"Would you rather I went?" asked the girl. Mr Briggerland would much rather that she had undertaken the disagreeable experience which lay before him, but he dare not confess as much.

"You, my dear? Of course not! I would not allow you to have such an experience. No, no, I don't mind it a bit."

Nevertheless, he tossed down two long glasses of brandy before he left.

His car set him down before the iron gates of a squat and ugly stucco building, surrounded by high walls, and the uniformed attendant, having examined his credentials, admitted him.

He had to wait a little while before a second attendant arrived to conduct him to the medical superintendent, an elderly man who did not seem overwhelmed with joy at the honour Mr Briggerland was paying him.

"I'm sorry I shan't be able to show you round, Mr Briggerland," he said. "I have an engagement in town, but my assistant, Dr Carew, will conduct you over the asylum and give you all the information you require. This, of course, as you know, is a private institution. I should have thought you would have got more material for your book in one of the big public asylums. The people who are sent to Norwood, you know, are not the mild cases, and you will see some rather terrible sights. You are prepared for that?"

Mr Briggerland nodded. He was prepared to the extent of two full noggins of brandy. Moreover, he was well aware that Norwood was the asylum to which the more dangerous of lunatics were transferred.

Dr Carew proved to be a young and enthusiastic alienist whose heart and soul was in his work.

"I suppose you are prepared to see jumpy things," he said with a smile, as he conducted Mr Briggerland along a stone-vaulted corridor.

He opened a steel gate, the bars of which were encased with thick layers of rubber, crossed a grassy plot (there were no stone-flagged paths at Norwood) and entered one of the three buildings which constituted the asylum proper.

It was a harrowing, heart-breaking, and to some extent, a disappointing experience for Mr Briggerland. True, his heart did not break, because it was made of infrangible material, and his disappointment was counterbalanced by a certain vague relief.

At the end of two hours' inspection they were standing out on the big playing fields, watching the less violent of the patients wandering aimlessly about. Except one, they were unattended by keepers, but in the case of this one man, two stalwart uniformed men walked on either side of him.

"Who is he?" asked Briggerland.

"That is rather a sad case," said the alienist cheerfully. He had pointed out many "sad cases" in the same bright manner. "He's a doctor and a genuine homicide. Luckily they detected him before he did any mischief or he would have been in Broadmoor."

"Aren't you ever afraid of these men escaping?" asked Mr Briggerland.

"You asked that before," said the doctor in surprise. "No. You see, an insane asylum is not like a prison; to make a good getaway from prison you have to have outside assistance. Nobody wants to help a lunatic escape, otherwise it would be easier than getting out of prison, because we have no patrols in the grounds, the wards can be opened from the outside without a key and the night patrol who visits the wards every half-hour has no time for any other observation. Would you like to talk to Dr Thun?"

Mr Briggerland hesitated only for a second.

"Yes," he said huskily.

There was nothing in the appearance of the patient to suggest that he was in any way dangerous. A fair, bearded man, with pale blue eyes, he held out his hand impulsively to the visitor, and after a momentary hesitation, Mr Briggerland took it and found his hand in a grip like a vice. The two attendants exchanged glances with the asylum doctor and strolled off.

"I think you can talk to him without fear," said the doctor in a low voice, not so low, however, that the patient did not hear it, for he laughed.

"Without fear, favour or prejudice, eh? Yes, that was how they swore the officers at my court martial."

"The doctor was the general who was responsible for the losses at Caperetto," explained Dr Carew. "That was where the Italians lost so heavily."

Thun nodded.

"Of course, I was perfectly innocent," he explained to Briggerland seriously, and taking the visitor's arm he strolled across the field, the doctor and the two attendants following at a distance. Mr Briggerland breathed a little more quickly as he felt the strength of the patient's biceps.

"My conviction," said Dr Thun seriously, "was due to the fact that women were sitting on the court martial, which is, of course, against all regulations."

"Certainly," murmured Mr Briggerland.

"Keeping me here," Thun went on, "is part of the plot of the Italian government. Naturally, they do not wish me to get at my enemies, who I have every reason to believe are in London."

Mr Briggerland drew a long breath.

"They are in London," he said a little hoarsely. "I happen to know where they are."

"Really?" said the other easily, and then a cloud passed over his face and he shook his head.

"They are safe from my vengeance," he said a little sadly. "As long as they keep me in this place pretending that I am mad, there is no possible chance for me."

The visitor looked round and saw that the three men who were following were out of earshot.

"Suppose I came tomorrow night," he said, lowering his voice, "and helped you to get away? What is your ward?"

"No. 6," said the other in the same tone. His eyes were blazing.

"Do you think you will remember?" asked Briggerland.

Thun nodded.

"You will come tomorrow night – No. 6, the first cubicle on the left," he whispered, "you will not fail me? If I thought you'd fail me – " His eyes lit up again.

"I shall not fail you," said Mr Briggerland hastily. "When the clock strikes twelve you may expect me."

"You must be Marshal Foch," murmured Thun, and then, with all a madman's cunning, changed the conversation as the doctor and attendants, who had noticed his excitement, drew nearer. "Believe me,

Mr Briggerland," he went on airily, "the strategy of the Allies was at fault until I took up the command of the army…"

Ten minutes later Mr Briggerland was in his car driving homeward, a little breathless, more than a little terrified at the unpleasant task he had set himself; jubilant, too, at his amazing success.

Jean had said he might have to visit a dozen asylums before he found his opportunity and the right man, and he had succeeded at the first attempt. Yet − he shuddered at the picture he conjured − that climb over the high wall (he had already located the ward, for he had followed the General and the attendants and had seen him safely put away), the midnight association with a madman…

He burst in upon Jean with his news.

"At the first attempt, my dear, what do you think of that?" His dark face glowed with almost childish pride, and she looked at him with a half-smile.

"I thought you would," she said quietly. "That's the rough work done, at any rate."

"The rough work!" he said indignantly.

She nodded.

"Half the difficulty is going to be to cover up your visit to the asylum, because this man is certain to mention your name, and it will not all be dismissed as the imagination of a madman. Now I think I will make my promised call upon Mrs Meredith."

13

There was one thing which rather puzzled and almost piqued Lydia Meredith, and that was the failure of Jean Briggerland's prophecy to materialise. Jean had said half jestingly that Jack Glover would be a frequent visitor at the flat; in point of fact, he did not come at all. Even when she visited the offices of Rennett, Glover and Simpson, it was Mr Rennett who attended to her, and Jack was invisible. Mr Rennett sometimes explained that he was at the courts, for Jack did all the court work, sometimes that he had gone home.

She caught a glimpse of him once as she was driving past the Law Courts in the Strand. He was standing on the pavement talking to a bewigged counsel, so possibly Mr Rennett had not stated more than the truth when he said that the young man's time was mostly occupied by the processes of litigation.

She was curious enough to look through the telephone directory to discover where he lived. There were about fifty Glovers, and ten of these were John Glovers, and she was enough of a woman to call up six of the most likely only to discover that her Mr Glover was not amongst them. She did not know till later that his full name was Bertram John Glover, or she might have found his address without difficulty.

Mrs Morgan had now arrived, to Lydia's infinite relief, and had taken control of the household affairs. The new maid was as perfect as a new maid could be, and but for the nightly intrusion of the taciturn Jaggs, to whom, for some reason, Mrs Morgan took a liking, the current of her domestic life ran smoothly.

She was already becoming accustomed to the possession of wealth. The habit of being rich is one of the easiest acquired, and she found herself negotiating for a little house in Curzon Street and a more pretentious establishment in Somerset, with a sang-froid which astonished and frightened her.

The purchase and arrival of her first car, and the engagement of her chauffeur, had been a thrilling experience. It was incredible, too, that her new bankers should, without hesitation, deliver to her enormous sums of money at the mere affixing of her signature to an oblong slip of paper.

She had even got over the panic feeling which came to her on her first few visits to the bank. On these earlier occasions she had felt rather like an inexpert forger, who was endeavouring to get money by false pretence, and it was both a relief and a wonder to her when the nonchalant cashier thrust thick wads of banknotes under the grille, without so much as sending for a policeman.

"It's a lovely flat," said Jean Briggerland, looking round the pink drawing-room approvingly, "but of course, my dear, this is one that was already furnished for you. I'm dying to see what you will make of your own home when you get one."

She had telephoned that morning to Lydia saying that she was paying a call, asking if it was convenient, and the two girls were alone.

"It is a nice flat, and I shall be sorry to leave it," agreed Lydia. "It is so extraordinarily quiet. I sleep like a top. There is no noise to disturb one, except that there was rather an unpleasant happening the other morning."

"What was that?" asked Jean, stirring her tea.

"I don't know really what happened," said Lydia. "I heard an awful groaning very early in the morning and I got up and looked out of the window. There were two men in the courtyard. One, I think, had hurt himself very badly. I never discovered what happened."

"They must have been workmen, I should think," said Jean, "or else they were drunk. Personally, I have never liked taking furnished flats," she went on. "One always breaks things, and there's such a big bill to pay at the end. And then I always lose the keys. One usually has two or three. You should be very careful about that, my dear, they make an enormous charge for lost keys," she prattled on.

"I think the house agent gave me three," said Lydia. She walked to her little secretaire, opened it and pulled out a drawer.

"Yes, three," she said, "there is one here, one I carry, and Mrs Morgan has one."

"Have you seen Jack Glover lately?"

Jean never pursued an enquiry too far, by so much as one syllable.

"No, I haven't seen him," smiled Lydia. "You weren't a good prophet."

"I expect he is busy," said the girl carelessly. "I think I could like Jack awfully – if he hadn't such a passion for ordering people about. How careless of me!" She had tipped over her teacup and its contents were running across the little tea table. She pulled out her handkerchief quickly and tried to stop the flow.

"Oh, please, please don't spoil your beautiful handkerchief," said Lydia, rising hurriedly, "I will get a duster."

She ran out of the room and was back almost immediately, to find Jean standing with her back to the secretaire examining the ruins of her late handkerchief with a smile.

"Let me put your handkerchief in water or it will be stained," said Lydia, putting out her hand.

"I would rather do it myself," laughed Jean Briggerland, and pushed the handkerchief into her bag.

There were many reasons why Lydia should not handle that flimsy piece of cambric and lace, the most important of which was the key which Jean had taken from the secretaire in Lydia's absence, and had rolled inside the tea-stained handkerchief.

A few days later Mr Bertram John Glover interviewed a high official at Scotland Yard, and the interview was not a particularly satisfactory one to the lawyer. It might have been worse, had not the police commissioner been a friend of Jack's partner.

The official listened patiently whilst the lawyer, with professional skill, marshalled all his facts, attaching to them the suspicions which had matured to convictions.

"I have sat in this chair for twenty-five years," said the head of the CID, "and I have heard stories which beat the best and the worst of detective stories hollow. I have listened to cranks, amateur detectives, crooks, parsons and expert fictionists, but never in my experience have I ever heard anything quite so improbable as your theory. It happens that I have met Briggerland and I've met his daughter too, and a more beautiful girl I don't think it has been my pleasure to meet."

Jack groaned.

"Aren't you feeling well?" asked the chief unpleasantly.

"I'm all right, sir," said Jack, "only I'm so tired of hearing about Jean Briggerland's beauty. It doesn't seem a very good argument to oppose to the facts – "

"Facts!" said the other scornfully. "What facts have you given us?"

"The fact of the Briggerlands' history," said Jack desperately. "Briggerland was broke when he married Miss Meredith under the impression that he would get a fortune with his wife. He has lived by his wits all his life, and until this girl was about fifteen, they were existing in a state of poverty. They lived in a tiny house in Ealing, the rent of which was always in arrears, and then Briggerland became acquainted with a rich Australian of middle age who was crazy about his daughter. The rich Australian died suddenly."

"From an overdose of veronal," said the chief. "It was established at the inquest – I got all the documents out after I received your letter – that he was in the habit of taking veronal. You suggest he was murdered. If he was, for what? He left the girl about six thousand pounds."

"Briggerland thought she was going to get it all," said Jack.

"That is conjecture," interrupted the chief. "Go on."

"Briggerland moved up west," Jack went on, "and when the girl was seventeen she made the acquaintance of a man named Gunnesbury, who went just as mad about her. Gunnesbury was a midland merchant with a wife and family. He was so infatuated with her that he collected all the loose money he could lay his hands on – some twenty-five thousand pounds – and bolted to the Continent. The girl was supposed to have gone on ahead, and he was to join her at Calais. He never reached Calais. The theory was that he jumped overboard. His body was found and brought in to Dover, but there was none of the money in his possession that he had drawn from the Midland Bank."

"That is a theory, too," said the chief, shaking his head. "The identity of the girl was never established. It was known that she was a friend of Gunnesbury's, but there was proof that she was in London on the night of his death. It was a clear case of suicide."

"A year later," Jack went on, "she forced a meeting with Meredith, her cousin. His father had just died – Jim had come back from Central Africa to put things in order. He was not a woman's man, and was a grave, retiring sort of fellow, who had no other interest in life than his shooting. The story of Meredith you know."

"And is that all?" asked the chief politely.

"All the facts I can gather. There must be other cases which are beyond the power of the investigator to unearth."

"And what do you expect me to do?"

Jack smiled.

"I don't expect you to do anything," he said frankly. "You are not exactly supporting my views with enthusiasm."

The chief rose, a signal that the interview was at an end.

"I'd like to help you if you had any real need for help," he said. "But when you come to me and tell me that Miss Briggerland, a girl whose innocence shows in her face, is a heartless criminal and murderess, and a conspirator – why, Mr Glover, what do you expect me to say?"

"I expect you to give adequate protection to Mrs Meredith," said Jack sharply. "I expect you, sir, to remember that I've warned you that Mrs Meredith may die one of those accidental deaths in which Mr and Miss Briggerland specialise. I'm going to put my warning in black and white, and if anything happens to Lydia Meredith, there is going to be serious trouble on the Thames Embankment."

The chief touched a bell, and a constable came in.

"Show Mr Glover the way out," he said stiffly.

Jack had calmed down considerably by the time he reached the Thames Embankment, and was inclined to be annoyed with himself for losing his temper.

He stopped a newsboy, took a paper from his hand, and, hailing a cab, drove to his office.

There was little in the early edition save the sporting news, but on the front page a paragraph arrested his eye.

DANGEROUS LUNATIC AT LARGE

The Medical Superintendent at Norwood Asylum reports that Dr Algernon John Thun, an inmate of the asylum, escaped last night, and is believed to be at large in the neighbourhood. Search parties have been organised, but no trace of the man has been found. He is known to have homicidal tendencies, a fact which renders his immediate recapture a very urgent necessity.

There followed a description of the wanted man. Jack turned to another part of the paper, and dismissed the paragraph from his mind.

His partner, however, was to bring the matter up at lunch. Norwood Asylum was near Dulwich, and Mr Rennett was pardonably concerned.

"The womenfolk at my house are scared to death," he said at lunch. "They won't go out at night, and they keep all the doors locked. How did your interview with the commissioner go on?"

"We parted the worst of friends," said Jack, "and, Rennett, the next man who talks to me about Jean Briggerland's beautiful face is going to be killed dead through it, even though I have to take a leaf from her book and employ the grisly Jaggs to do it."

14

That night the "grisly Jaggs" was later than usual. Lydia heard him shuffling along the passage, and presently the door of his room closed with a click. She was sitting at the piano, and had stopped playing at the sound of his knock, and when Mrs Morgan came in to announce his arrival, she closed the piano and swung round on the music stool, a look of determination on her delicate face.

"He's come, miss."

"And for the last time," said Lydia ominously. "Mrs Morgan, I can't stand that weird old gentleman any longer. He has got on my nerves so that I could scream when I think of him."

"He's not a bad old gentleman," excused Mrs Morgan.

"I'm not so worried about his moral character, and I dare say that it is perfectly blameless," said Lydia determinedly, "but I have written a note to Mr Glover to tell him that I really must dispense with his services."

"What's he here for, miss?" asked Mrs Morgan.

Her curiosity had been aroused, but this was the first time she had given it expression.

"He's here because – " Lydia hesitated, "well, because Mr Glover thinks I ought to have a man in the house to look after me."

"Why, miss?" asked the startled woman.

"You'd better ask Mr Glover that question," said Lydia grimly.

She was beginning to chafe under the sense of restraint. She was being "school-marmed" she thought. No girl likes the ostentatious protection of the big brother or the headmistress. The soul of the schoolgirl yearns to break from the "crocodile" in which she is marched to church and to school, and this sensation of being marshalled and ordered about, and of living her life according to a third person's programme, and that third person a man, irked her horribly.

Old Jaggs was the outward and visible sign of Jack Glover's unwarranted authority, and slowly there was creeping into her mind a suspicion that Jean Briggerland might not have been mistaken when she spoke of Jack's penchant for "ordering people about".

Life was growing bigger for her. She had broken down the barriers which had confined her to a narrow promenade between office and home. The hours which she had had to devote to work were now entirely free, and she could sketch or paint whenever the fancy took her – which was not very often, though she promised herself a period of hard work when once she was settled down.

Toward the good-looking young lawyer her point of view had shifted. She hardly knew herself how she regarded him. He irritated, and yet in some indefinable way, pleased her. His sincerity – ? She did not doubt his sincerity. She admitted to herself that she wished he would call a little more frequently than he did. He might have persuaded her that Jaggs was a necessary evil, but he hadn't even taken the trouble to come. Therefore – but this she did not admit – Jaggs must go.

"I don't think the old gentleman's quite right in his head, you know, sometimes," said Mrs Morgan.

"Why ever not, Mrs Morgan?" asked the girl in surprise.

"I often hear him sniggering to himself as I go past his door. I suppose he stays in his room all night, miss?"

"He doesn't," said the girl emphatically, "and that's why he's going. I heard him in the passage at two o'clock this morning; I'm getting into such a state of nerves that the slightest sound awakens me. He had his boots off and was creeping about in his stockings, and when I went out and switched the light on he bolted back to his room. I can't have that sort of thing going on, and I won't! It's altogether too creepy!"

Mrs Morgan agreed.

Lydia had not been out in the evening for several days, she remembered, as she began to undress for the night. The weather had been unpleasant, and to stay in the warm, comfortable flat was no great hardship. Even if she had gone out, Jaggs would have accompanied her, she thought ironically.

And then she had a little twinge of conscience, remembering that Jaggs' presence on a memorable afternoon had saved her from destruction.

She wondered for the twentieth time what was old Jaggs' history, and where Jack had found him. Once she had been tempted to ask Jaggs himself, but the old man had fenced with the question, and had talked vaguely of having worked in the country, and she was as wise as she had been before.

But she must get rid of old Jaggs, she thought, as she switched off the light and kicked out the innumerable water bottles, with which Mrs Morgan, in mistaken kindness, had encumbered the bed…old Jaggs must go…he was a nuisance…

She woke with a start from a dreamless sleep. The clock in the hall was striking three. She realised this subconsciously. Her eyes were fixed on the window, which was open at the bottom. Mrs Morgan had pulled it down at the top, but now it was wide open, and her heart began to thump, thump, rapidly. Jaggs! He was her first thought. She would never have believed that she could have thought of that old man with such a warm glow of thankfulness. There was nothing to be seen. The storm of the early night had passed over, and a faint light came into the room from the waning moon. And then she saw the curtains move, and opened her mouth to scream, but fear had paralysed her voice, and she lay staring at the hangings, incapable of movement or sound. As she watched the curtain she saw it move again, and a shape appeared faintly against the gloomy background.

The spell was broken. She swung herself out of the opposite side of the bed, and raced to the door, but the man was before her. Before she could scream, a big hand gripped her throat and flung her back against the rail of the bed.

74

Horrified she stared into the cruel face that leered down at her, and felt the grip tighten. And then as she looked into the face she saw a sudden grimace, and sensed the terror in his eyes. The hand relaxed; he bubbled something thickly and fell sideways against the bed. And now she saw. A man had come through the doorway, a tall man, with a fair beard and eyes that danced with insane joy.

He came slowly toward her, wiping on his cuff the long-handled knife that had sent her assailant to the floor.

He was mad. She knew it instinctively, and remembered in a hazy, confused way, a paragraph she had read about an escaped lunatic. She tried to dash past him to the open door, but he caught her in the crook of his left arm, and pressed her to him, towering head and shoulders over her.

"You have no right to sit on a court martial, madam," he said with uncanny politeness, and at that moment the light in the room was switched on and Jaggs appeared in the doorway, his bearded lips parted in an ugly grin, a long-barrelled pistol in his left hand.

"Drop your knife," he said, "or I'll drop you."

The mad doctor turned his head slowly and frowned at the intruder.

"Good morning, General," he said calmly. "You came in time," and he threw the knife on to the ground. "We will try her according to regulations!"

15

A TRAGIC AFFAIR IN THE WEST END
MAD DOCTOR WOUNDS A BURGLAR IN A
SOCIETY WOMAN'S BEDROOM

There was an extraordinary and tragic sequel to the escape of Dr Thun from Norwood Asylum, particulars of which appeared in our early edition of yesterday. This morning at four o'clock, in answer to a telephone call, Detective-Sergeant Miller, accompanied by another officer, went to 84, Cavendish Mansions, a flat occupied by Mrs Meredith, and there found and took into custody Dr Algernon Thun, who had escaped from Norwood Asylum. In the room was also found a man named Hoggins, a person well known to the police. It appears that Hoggins had effected an entrance into Mrs Meredith's flat, descending from the roof by means of a rope, making his way into the premises through the window of Mrs Meredith's bedroom. Whilst there he was detected by Mrs Meredith, who would undoubtedly have been murdered had not Dr Thun, who, in some mysterious manner, had gained admission to the flat, intervened. In the struggle that followed the doctor, who is suffering from the delusion of persecution, severely wounded the man, who is not expected to live. He then turned his attention to the lady. Happily an old man who works at the flat, who was sleeping on the premises at the time, was roused by the sound of the struggle, and succeeded in releasing the lady from the maniacal grasp of the intruder. The wounded burglar was removed to hospital and the lunatic was taken to the police station and was afterwards sent under a strong guard to the asylum from whence he had escaped. He made a rambling statement to the police to the effect that General Foch had assisted his escape and had directed him to the home of his persecutors.

Jean Briggerland put down the paper and laughed.

"It is nothing to snigger about," growled Briggerland savagely.

"If I didn't laugh I should do something more emotional," said the girl coolly. "To think that that fool should go back and make the attempt single-handed. I never imagined that."

"Faire tells me that he's not expected to live," said Mr Briggerland. He rubbed his baldhead irritably. "I wonder if that lunatic is going to talk?"

"What does it matter if he does?" said the girl impatiently.

"You said the other day − " he began.

"The other day it mattered, my dear father. Today nothing matters very much. I think we have got well out of it. I ignored all the lessons which my textbook teaches when I entrusted work to other hands. Jaggs," she said softly.

"Eh?" said the father.

"I'm repeating a well-beloved name," she smiled and rose, folding her serviette. "I am going for a long run in the country. Would you like to come? Mordon is very enthusiastic about the new car, the bill for which, by the way, came in this morning. Have we any money?"

"A few thousands," said her father, rubbing his chin. "Jean, we shall have to sell something unless things brighten."

Jean's lips twitched, but she said nothing.

On her way to the open road she called at Cavendish Mansions, and was neither surprised nor discomfited to discover that Jack Glover was there.

"My dear," she said, warmly clasping both the girl's hands in hers, "I was so shocked when I read the news! How terrible it must have been for you."

Lydia was looking pale, and there were dark shadows under her eyes, but she treated the matter cheerfully.

"I've just been trying to explain to Mr Glover what happened. Unfortunately, the wonderful Jaggs is not here. He knows more about it than I, for I collapsed in the most feminine way."

"How did he get in – I mean this madman?" asked the girl.

"Through the door."

It was Jack who answered.

"It is the last way in the world a lunatic would enter a flat, isn't it? He came in with a key, and he was brought here by somebody who struck a match to make sure it was the right number."

"He might have struck the match himself," said Jean, "but you're so clever that you would not say a thing like that unless you had proof."

"We found two matches in the hall outside," said Jack, "and when Dr Thun was searched no matches were found on him, and I have since learnt that, like most homicidal lunatics, he had a horror of fire in any form. The doctor to whom I have been talking is absolutely sure that he would not have struck the match himself. Oh, by the way, Miss Briggerland, your father met this unfortunate man. I understand he paid a visit to the asylum a few days ago?"

"Yes, he did," she answered without hesitation. "He was talking about him this morning. You see, father has been making a tour of the asylums. He is writing a book about such things. Father was horrified when he heard the man had escaped, because the doctor told him that he was a particularly dangerous lunatic. But who would have imagined he would have turned up here?"

Her big, sad eyes were fixed on Jack as she shook her head in wonder.

"If one had read that in a book one would never have believed it, would one?"

"And the man Hoggins," said Jack, who did not share her wonder. "He was by way of being an acquaintance of yours, a member of your father's club, wasn't he?"

She knit her brows.

"I don't remember the name, but if he is a very bad character," she said with a little smile, "I should say distinctly that he was a member of father's club! Poor daddy, I don't think he will ever regenerate the East End."

"I don't think he will," agreed Jack heartily. "The question is, whether the East End will ever regenerate him."

A slow smile dawned on her face.

"How unkind!" she said, mockery in her eyes now. "I wonder why you dislike him so. He is so very harmless, really. My dear," she turned to the girl with a gesture of helplessness. "I am afraid that even in this affair Mr Glover is seeing my sinister influence!"

"You're the most unsinister person I have ever met, Jean," laughed Lydia, "and Mr Glover doesn't really think all these horrid things."

"Doesn't he?" said Jean softly, and Jack saw that she was shaking with laughter.

There was a certain deadly humour in the situation which tickled him too, and he grinned.

"I wish to heaven you'd get married and settle down, Miss Briggerland," he said incautiously.

It was her chance. She shook her head, the lips drooped, the eyes again grew moist with the pain she could call to them at will.

"I wish I could," she said in a tone a little above a whisper, "but, Jack, I could never marry you, never!"

She left Jack Glover bereft of speech, totally incapable of arousing so much as a moan.

Lydia, returning from escorting her visitor to the door, saw his embarrassment and checked his impulsive explanation a little coldly.

"I – I believed you when you said it wasn't true, Mr Glover," she said, and there was a reproach in her tone for which she hated herself afterwards.

16

Lydia had promised to go to the theatre that night with Mrs Cole-Mortimer, and she was glad of the excuse to leave her tragic home.

Mrs Cole-Mortimer, who was not lavish in the matter of entertainments that cost money, had a box, and although Lydia had seen the piece before (it was in fact the very play she had attended to sketch dresses on the night of her adventure) it was a relief to sit in silence, which her hostess, with singular discretion, did not attempt to disturb.

It was during the last act that Mrs Cole-Mortimer gave her an invitation which she accepted joyfully.

"I've got a house at Cap Martin," said Mrs Cole-Mortimer. "It is only a tiny place, but I think you would rather like it. I hate going to the Riviera alone, so if you care to come as my guest, I shall be most happy to chaperon you. They are bringing my yacht down to Monaco, so we ought to have a really good time."

Lydia accepted the yacht and the house as she had accepted the invitation – without question. That the yacht had been chartered that morning and the house hired by telegram on the previous day, she could not be expected to guess. For all she knew, Mrs Cole-Mortimer might be a very wealthy woman, and in her wildest dreams she did not imagine that Jean Briggerland had provided the money for both.

It had not been a delicate negotiation, because Mrs Cole-Mortimer had the skin of a pachyderm.

Years later Lydia discovered that the woman lived on borrowed money, money which never could and never would be repaid, and which the borrower had no intention of refunding.

A hint dropped by Jean that there was somebody on the Riviera whom she desired to meet, without her father's knowledge, accompanied by the plain statement that she would pay all expenses, was quite sufficient for Mrs Cole-Mortimer, and she had fallen in with her patron's views as readily as she had agreed to pose as a friend of Meredith's. To do her justice, she had the faculty of believing in her own invention, and she was quite satisfied that James Meredith had been a great personal friend of hers, just as she would believe that the house on the Riviera and the little steam yacht had been procured out of her own purse.

It was harder for her, however, to explain the great system which she was going to work in Monte Carlo and which was to make everybody's fortune.

Lydia, who was no gambler and only mildly interested in games of chance, displayed so little evidence of interest in the scheme that Mrs Cole-Mortimer groaned her despair, not knowing that she was expected to do no more than stir the soil for the crop which Jean Briggerland would plant and reap.

They went on to supper at one of the clubs, and Lydia thought with amusement of poor old Jaggs, who apparently took his job very seriously indeed.

Again her angle of vision had shifted, and her respect for the old man had overcome any annoyance his uncouth presence brought to her.

As she alighted at the door of the club she looked round, half expecting to see him. The club entrance was up a side street off Leicester Square, an ill-lit thoroughfare which favoured Mr Jaggs' retiring methods, but there was no sign of him, and she did not wait in the drizzling night to make any closer inspection.

Mrs Cole-Mortimer had not disguised the possibility of Jean Briggerland being at the club, and they found her with a gay party of young people, sitting in one of the recesses. Jean made a place for the girl by her side and introduced her to half a dozen people whose names Lydia did not catch, and never afterwards remembered.

Mr Marcus Stepney, however, that sleek, dark man, who bowed over her hand and seemed as though he were going to kiss it, she had met before, and her second impression of him was even less favourable than the first.

"Do you dance?" asked Jean.

A jazz band was playing an infectious two-step. At the girl's nod Jean beckoned one of her party, a tall, handsome boy who throughout the subsequent dance babbled into Lydia's ear an incessant paean in praise of Jean Briggerland.

Lydia was amused.

"Of course she is very beautiful," she said in answer to the interminable repetition of his question. "I think she's lovely."

"That's what I say," said the young man, whom she discovered was Lord Stoker. "The most amazingly beautiful creature on the earth, I think."

"Of course you're awfully good-looking, too," he blundered, and Lydia laughed aloud.

"But she's got enemies," said the young man viciously, "and if ever I meet that infernal cad, Glover, he'll be sorry."

The smile left Lydia's face.

"Mr Glover is a friend of mine," she said a little quickly.

"Sorry," he mumbled, "but – "

"Does Miss Briggerland say he is so very bad?"

"Of course not. She never says a word against him really." His lordship hastened to exonerate his idol. "She just says she doesn't know how long she's going to stand his persecutions. It breaks one's heart to see how sad this – your friend makes her."

Lydia was a very thoughtful girl for the rest of the evening; she was beginning in a hazy way to see things which she had not seen before. Of course Jean never said anything against Jack Glover. And yet she had succeeded in arousing this youth to fury against the lawyer, and Lydia realised, with a sense of amazement, that Jean had also made her feel bad about Jack. And yet she had said nothing but sweet things.

When she got back to the flat that night she found that Mr Jaggs had not been there all the evening. He came in a few minutes after her, wrapped up in an old army coat, and from his appearance she gathered that he had been standing out in the rain and sleet the whole of the evening.

"Why, Jaggs," she said impulsively, "wherever have you been?"

"Just dodging round, miss," he grunted. "Having a look at the little ducks in the pond."

"You've been outside the theatre, and you've been waiting outside Niro's Club," she said accusingly.

"Don't know it, miss," he said. "One theayter is as much like another one to me."

"You must take your things off and let Mrs Morgan dry your clothes," she insisted, but he would not hear of this, compromising only with stripping his sodden great coat.

He disappeared into his dark room, there to ruminate upon such matters as appeared of interest to him. A bed had been placed for him, but only once had he slept on it.

After the flat grew still and the last click of the switch told that the last light had been extinguished, he opened the door softly, and, carrying a chair in his hand, he placed this gently with its back to the front door, and there he sat and dozed throughout the night. When Lydia woke the next morning he was gone as usual.

17

Lydia had plenty to occupy her days. The house in Curzon Street had been bought and she had been a round of furnishers, paper-hangers and fitters of all variety.

The trip to the Riviera came at the right moment. She could leave Mrs Morgan in charge and come back to her new home, which was to be ready in two months.

Amongst other things, the problem of the watchful Mr Jaggs would be settled automatically.

She spoke to him that night when he came. "By the way, Mr Jaggs, I am going to the South of France next week."

"A pretty place by all accounts," volunteered Mr Jaggs.

"A lovely place – by all accounts," repeated Lydia with a smile. "And you're going to have a holiday, Mr Jaggs. By the way, what am I to pay you?"

"The gentleman pays me, miss," said Mr Jaggs with a sniff. "The lawyer gentleman."

"Well, he must continue paying you whilst I am away," said the girl. "I am very grateful to you and I want to give you a little present before I go. Is there anything you would like, Mr Jaggs?"

Mr Jaggs rubbed his beard, scratched his head and thought he would like a pipe.

"Though bless you, miss, I don't want any present."

"You shall have the best pipe I can buy," said the girl. "It seems very inadequate."

"I'd rather have a briar, miss," said old Jaggs mistakenly.

He was on duty until the morning she left, and although she rose early she had gone. She was disappointed, for she had not given him the handsome case of pipes she had bought, and she wanted to thank him. She felt she had acted rather meanly towards him. She owed her life to him twice.

"Didn't you see him go?" she asked Mrs Morgan.

"No, miss," the stout housekeeper shook her head. "I was up at six and he'd gone then, but he'd left his chair in the passage – I've got an idea that's where he slept, miss, if he slept at all."

"Poor old man," said the girl gently. "I haven't been very kind to him, have I? And I do owe him such a lot."

"Maybe he'll turn up again," said Mrs Morgan hopefully. She had the mother feeling for the old, which is one of the beauties of her class, and she regretted Lydia's absence probably as much because it would entail the disappearance of old Jaggs as for the loss of her mistress. But old Jaggs did not turn up. Lydia hoped to see him at the station, hovering on the outskirts of the crowd in his furtive way, but she was disappointed.

She left by the eleven o'clock train, joining Mrs Cole-Mortimer on the station. That lady had arranged to spend a day in Paris, and the girl was not sorry, after a somewhat bad crossing of the English Channel, that she had not to continue her journey through the night.

The South of France was to be a revelation to her. She had no conception of the extraordinary change of climate and vegetation that could be experienced in one country.

She passed from a drizzly, bedraggled Paris into a land of sunshine and gentle breezes; from the bare sullen lands of the Champagne, into a country where flowers grew by the side of the railway, and that in February; to a semi-tropic land, fragrant with flowers, to white beaches by a blue, lazy sea and a sky over all unflecked by clouds.

It took her breath away, the beauty of it; and the sense and genial warmth of it. The trees laden with lemons, the wisteria on the walls, the white dust on the road, and the glory of the golden mimosa that scented the air with its rare and lovely perfume.

They left the train at Nice and drove along the Grande Corniche. Mrs Cole-Mortimer had a call to make in Monte Carlo and the girl sat back in the car and drank in the beauty of this delicious spot, whilst her hostess interviewed the house agent.

Surely the place must be kept under glass. It looked so fresh and clean and free from stain.

The Casino disappointed her – it was a place of plaster and stucco, and did not seem built for permanent use.

They drove back part of the way they had come, on to the peninsula of Cap Martin, and she had a glimpse of beautiful villas between the pines and queer little roads that led into mysterious dells. Presently the car drew up before a good-looking house (even Mrs Cole-Mortimer was surprised into an expression of her satisfaction at the sight of it).

Lydia, who thought that this was Mrs Cole-Mortimer's own demesne, was delighted.

"You are lucky to have a beautiful home like this, Mrs Cole-Mortimer," she said, "it must be heavenly living here."

The habit of wealth had not been so well acquired that she could realise that she also could have a beautiful house if she wished – she thought of that later. Nor did she expect to find Jean Briggerland there, and Mr Briggerland too, sitting on a big cane chair on the veranda overlooking the sea and smoking a cigar of peace.

Mrs Cole-Mortimer had been very careful to avoid all mention of Jean on the journey.

"Didn't I tell you they would be here?" she said in careless amazement. "Why, of course, dear Jean left two days before we did. It makes such a nice little party. Do you play bridge?"

Lydia did not play bridge, but was willing to be taught.

She spent the remaining hour of daylight exploring the grounds which led down to the road which fringed the sea.

She could look across at the lights already beginning to twinkle at Monte Carlo, to the white yachts lying off Monaco, and farther along the coast to a little cluster of lights that stood for Beaulieu.

"It is glorious," she said, drawing a long breath.

Mrs Cole-Mortimer, who had accompanied her in her stroll, purred the purr of the pleased patron whose protégée has been thankful for favours received.

Dinner was a gay meal, for Jean was in her brightest mood. She had a keen sense of fun and her sly little sallies, sometimes aimed at her father, sometimes at Lydia's expense, but more often directed at people in the social world, whose names were household words, kept Lydia in a constant gurgle of laughter.

Mrs Cole-Mortimer alone was nervous and ill at ease. She had learnt unpleasant news and was not sure whether she should tell the company or keep her secret to herself. In such dilemma, weak people take the most sensational course, and presently she dropped her bombshell.

"Celeste says that the gardener's little boy has malignant smallpox," she almost wailed.

Jean was telling a funny story to the girl who sat by her, and did not pause for so much as a second in her narrative. The effect on Mr Briggerland was, however, wholly satisfactory to Mrs Cole-Mortimer. He pushed back his chair and blinked at his "hostess".

"Smallpox?" he said in horror, "here – in Cap Martin? Good God, did you hear that, Jean?"

"Did I hear what?" she asked lazily, "about the gardener's little boy? Oh, yes. There has been quite an epidemic on the Italian Riviera, in fact they closed the frontier last week."

"But – but here!" spluttered Briggerland. Lydia could only look at him in open-eyed amazement. The big man's terror was pitiably apparent. The copper skin had turned a dirty grey, his lower lip was trembling like a frightened child's.

"Why not here?" said Jean coolly, "there is nothing to be scared about. Have you been vaccinated recently?" she turned to the girl, and Lydia shook her head.

"Not since I was a baby – and then I believe the operation was not a success."

"Anyway, the child is isolated in the cottage and they are taking him to Nice tonight," said Jean. "Poor little fellow! Even his own mother has deserted him. Are you going to the Casino?" she asked.

"I don't know," replied Lydia. "I'm very tired but I should love to go."

"Take her, father – and you go, Margaret. By the time you return the infection will be removed."

"Won't you come too?" asked Lydia.

"No, I'll stay at home tonight. I turned my ankle today and it is rather stiff. Father!"

This time her voice was sharp, menacing almost, thought Lydia, and Mr Briggerland made an heroic attempt to recover his self-possession.

"Cer – certainly, my dear – I shall be delighted – er – delighted."

He saw her alone whilst Lydia was changing in her lovely big dressing room, overlooking the sea.

"Why didn't you tell me there was smallpox in Cap Martin?" he demanded fretfully.

"Because I didn't know till Margaret relieved her mind at our expense," said his daughter coolly. "I had to say something. Besides, I'd heard one of the maids say that somebody's mother had deserted him – I fitted it in. What a funk you are, father!"

"I hate the very thought of disease," he growled. "Why aren't you coming with us – there is nothing the matter with your ankle?"

"Because I prefer to stay at home."

He looked at her suspiciously.

"Jean," he said in a milder voice, "hadn't we better let up on the girl for a bit – until that lunatic doctor affair has blown over?"

She reached out and took a gold case from his waistcoat pocket, extracted a cigarette and replaced the case before she spoke.

"We can't afford to 'let up' as you call it, for a single hour. Do you realise that any day her lawyer may persuade her to make a will leaving her money to a – a home for cats, or something equally untouchable? If there was no Jack Glover we could afford to wait months. And I'm less troubled about him than I am about the man

Jaggs. Father, you will be glad to learn that I am almost afraid of that freakish old man."

"Neither of them are here – " he began.

"Exactly," said Jean, "neither are here – Lydia had a telegram from him just before dinner asking if he could come to see her next week."

At this moment Lydia returned and Jean Briggerland eyed her critically.

"My dear, you look lovely," she said and kissed her.

Mr Briggerland's nose wrinkled, as it always did when his daughter shocked him.

18

Jean Briggerland waited until she heard the sound of the departing car sink to a faint hum, then she went up to her room, opened the bureau and took out a long and tightly fitting dust coat that she wore when she was motoring. She had seen a large bottle of peroxide in Mrs Cole-Mortimer's room. It probably contributed to the dazzling glories of Mrs Cole-Mortimer's hair, but it was also a powerful germicide. She soaked a big silk handkerchief in a basin of water, to which she added a generous quantity of the drug, and squeezing the handkerchief nearly dry, she knotted it loosely about her neck. A rubber bathing cap she pulled down over her head, and smiled at her queer reflection in the glass. Then she found a pair of kid gloves and drew them on.

She turned out the light and went softly down the carpeted stairs. The servants were at their dinner, and she opened the front door and crossed the lawn into a belt of trees, beyond which she knew, for she had been in the house two days, was the gardener's cottage.

A dim light burnt in one of the two rooms and the window was uncurtained. She saw the bed and its tiny occupant, but nobody else was in the room. The maid had said that the mother had deserted the little sufferer, but this was not quite true. The doctor had ordered the mother into isolation, and had sent a nurse from the infection hospital to take her place. That lady, at the moment, was waiting at the end of the avenue for the ambulance to arrive.

Jean opened the door and stepped in, pulling up the saturated handkerchief until it covered nose and mouth. The place was deserted,

and, without a moment's hesitation, she lifted the child, wrapped a blanket about it and crossed the lawn again. She went quietly up the stairs straight to Lydia's room. There was enough light from the dressing-room to see the bed, and unwrapping the blanket she pulled back the covers and laid him gently in the bed. The child unconscious. The hideous marks of the disease had developed with remarkable rapidity and he made no sound.

She sat down in a chair, waiting. Her almost inhuman calm was not ruffled by so much as a second's apprehension. She had provided for every contingency and was ready with a complete explanation, whatever happened.

Half an hour passed, and then rising, she wrapped the child in the blanket and carried him back to the cottage. She heard the purr of the motor and footsteps as she flitted back through the trees.

First she went to Lydia's room and straightened the bed, spraying the room with the faint perfume which she found on the dressing table; then she went back again into the garden, stripped off the dust coat, cap and handkerchief, rolling them into a bundle, which she thrust through the bars of an open window which she knew ventilated a cellar. Last of all she stripped her gloves and sent them after the bundle.

She heard the voices of the nurse and attendant as they carried the child to the ambulance.

"Poor little kid," she murmured, "I hope he gets better."

And, strangely enough, she meant it.

It had been a thrilling evening for Lydia, and she returned to the house at Cap Martin very tired, but very happy. She was seeing a new world, a world the like of which had never been revealed to her, and though she could have slept, and her head did nod in the car, she roused herself to talk it all over again with the sympathetic Jean.

Mrs Cole-Mortimer retired early. Mr Briggerland had gone up to bed the moment he returned, and Lydia would have been glad to have ended her conversation; since her head reeled with weariness, but Jean was very talkative, until – "My dear, if I don't go to bed I shall sleep on the table," smiled Lydia, rising and suppressing a yawn.

"I'm so sorry," said the penitent Jean.

She accompanied the girl upstairs, her arm about her waist, and left her at the door of her dressing room.

A maid had laid out her night things on a big settee (a little to Lydia's surprise) and she undressed quickly.

She opened the door of her bedroom, her hand was on a switch, when she was conscious of a faint and not unpleasant odour. It was a clean, pungent smell. "Disinfectant," said her brain mechanically. She turned on the light, wondering where it came from. And then as she crossed the room she came in sight of her bed and stopped, for it was saturated with water – water that dropped from the hanging coverlet, and made little pools on the floor. From the head of the bed to the foot there was not one dry place. Whosoever had done the work was thorough. Blankets, sheets, pillows were soddened, and from the soaked mass came a faint acrid aroma which she recognised, even before she saw on the floor an empty bottle labelled "Peroxide of Hydrogen".

She could only stand and stare. It was too late to arouse the household, and she remembered that there was a very comfortable settee in the dressing room with a rug and a pillow, and she went back.

A few minutes later she was fast asleep. Not so Miss Briggerland, who was sitting up in bed, a cigarette between her lips, a heavy volume on her knees, reading: "Such malignant cases are almost without exception rapidly fatal, sometimes so early that no sign of the characteristic symptoms appear at all," she read and, dropping the book on the floor, extinguished her cigarette on an alabaster tray, and settled herself to sleep. She was dozing when she remembered that she had forgotten to say her prayers.

"Oh, damn!" said Jean, getting out reluctantly to kneel on the cold floor by the side of the bed.

19

Her maid woke Jean Briggerland at eight o'clock the next morning.

"Oh, miss," she said, as she drew up the table for the chocolate, "have you heard about Mrs Meredith?"

Jean blinked open her eyes, slipped into her dressing jacket and sat up with a yawn.

"Have I heard about Mrs Meredith? Many times," she said.

"But what somebody did last night, miss?"

Jean was wide awake now.

"What has happened to Mrs Meredith?" she asked.

"Why, miss, somebody played a practical joke on her. Her bed's sopping."

"Sopping?" frowned the girl.

"Yes, miss," the woman nodded. "They must have poured buckets of water over it, and used up all Mrs Cole-Mortimer's peroxide, what she uses for keeping her hands nice."

Jean swung out of her bed and sat looking down at her tiny white feet.

"Where did Mrs Meredith sleep? Why didn't she wake us up?"

"She slept in the dressing room, miss. I don't suppose the young lady liked making a fuss."

"Who did it?"

"I don't know who did it. It's a silly kind of practical joke, and I know none of the maids would have dared, not the French ones."

Jean put her feet into her slippers, exchanged her jacket for a gown, and went on a tour of inspection.

Lydia was dressing in her room, and the sound of her fresh, young voice, as she carolled out of sheer love of life, came to the girl before she turned into the room.

One glance at the bed was sufficient. It was still wet, and the empty peroxide bottle told its own story.

Jean glanced at it thoughtfully as she crossed into the dressing room.

"Whatever happened last night, Lydia?"

Lydia turned at the voice.

"Oh, the bed you mean," she made a little face. "Heaven knows. It occurred to me this morning that some person, out of mistaken kindness, had started to disinfect the room – it was only this morning that I recalled the little boy who was ill – and had overdone it."

"They've certainly overdone it," said Jean grimly. "I wonder what poor Mrs Cole-Mortimer will say. You haven't the slightest idea – "

"Not the slightest idea," said Lydia, answering the unspoken question.

"I'll see Mrs Cole-Mortimer and get her to change your bed – there's another room you could have," suggested Jean.

She went back to her own apartment, bathed and dressed leisurely.

She found her father in the garden reading the *Niçoise*, under the shade of a bush, for the sun was not warm, but at that hour, blinding.

"I've changed my plans," she said without preliminary.

He looked up over his glasses.

"I didn't know you had any," he said with heavy humour.

"I intended going back to London and taking you with me," she said unexpectedly.

"Back to London?" he said incredulously. "I thought you were staying on for a month."

"I probably shall now," she said, pulling up a basket chair and sitting by his side. "Give me a cigarette."

"You're smoking a lot lately," he said as he handed his case to her.

"I know I am."

"Have your nerves gone wrong?"

She looked at him out of the corner of her eye and her lips curled.

"It wouldn't be remarkable if I inherited a little of your yellow streak," she said coolly, and he growled something under his breath.

"No, my nerves are all right, but a cigarette helps me to think."

"A yellow streak, have I?" Mr Briggerland was annoyed. "And I've been out since five o'clock this morning – " he stopped.

"Doing – what?" she asked curiously.

"Never mind," he said with a lofty gesture.

Thus they sat, busy with their own thoughts, for a quarter of an hour.

"Jean."

"Yes," she said without turning her head. "Don't you think we'd better give this up and get back to London? Lord Stoker is pretty keen on you."

"I'm not pretty keen on him," she said decidedly. "He has his regimental pay and £500 a year, two estates, mortgaged, no brains and a title – what is the use of his title to me? As much use as a coat of paint! Beside which, I am essentially democratic."

He chuckled, and there was another silence. "Do you think the lawyer is keen on the girl?"

"Jack Glover?"

Mr Briggerland nodded.

"I imagine he is," said Jean thoughtfully. "I like Jack – he's clever. He has all the moral qualities which one admires so much in the abstract. I could love Jack myself."

"Could he love you?" bantered her father.

"He couldn't," she said shortly. "Jack would be a happy man if he saw me stand in Jim Meredith's place in the Old Bailey. No, I have no illusion about Jack's affections."

"He's after Lydia's money I suppose," said Mr Briggerland, stroking his bald head.

"Don't be a fool," was the calm reply. "That kind of man doesn't worry about a girl's money. I wish Lydia was dead," she added without malice. "It would make things so easy and smooth."

Her father swallowed something.

"You shock me sometimes, Jean," he said, a statement which amused her.

"You're such a half-and-half man," she said with a note of contempt in her voice. "You were quite willing to benefit by Jim Meredith's death; you killed him as cold-bloodedly as you killed poor little Bulford, and yet you must whine and snivel whenever your deeds are put into plain language. What does it matter if Lydia dies now or in fifty years time?" she asked. "It would be different if she were immortal. You people attach so much importance to human life – the ancients, and the Japanese amongst the modern, are the only people who have the matter in true perspective. It is no more cruel to kill a human being than it is to cut the throat of a pig to provide you with bacon. There's hardly a dish at your table which doesn't represent wilful murder, and yet you never think of it, but because the man animal can talk and dresses himself or herself in queer animal and vegetable fabrics, and decorates the body with bits of metal and pieces of glittering quartz, you give its life a value which you deny to the cattle within your gates! Killing is a matter of expediency. Permissible if you call it war, terrible if you call it murder. To me it is just killing. If you are caught in the act of killing they kill you, and people say it is right to do so. The sacredness of human life is a slogan invented by cowards who fear death – as you do."

"Don't you, Jean?" he asked in a hushed voice.

"I fear life without money," she said quietly. "I fear long days of work for a callous, leering employer, and strap-hanging in a crowded tube on my way home to one miserable room and the cold mutton of yesterday. I fear getting up and making my own bed and washing my own handkerchiefs and blouses, and renovating last year's hats to make them look like this year's. I fear a poor husband and a procession of children, and doing the housework with an incompetent maid, or maybe without any at all. Those are the things I fear, Mr Briggerland."

She dusted the ash from her dress and got up.

"I haven't forgotten the life we lived at Ealing," she said significantly.

She looked across the bay to Monte Carlo glittering in the morning sunlight, to the green-capped head of Cap d'Ail, to Beaulieu, a jewel set in grey stone and shook her head.

" 'It is written'," she quoted sombrely and left him in the midst of the question he was asking. She strolled back to the house and joined Lydia who was looking radiantly beautiful in a new dress of silver grey charmeuse.

20

"Have you solved the mystery of the submerged bed?" smiled Jean.
Lydia laughed.

"I'm not probing too deeply into the matter," she said. "Poor Mrs Cole-Mortimer was terribly upset."

"She would be," said Jean. "It was her own eiderdown!"

This was the first hint Lydia had received that the house was rented furnished.

They drove into Nice that morning, and Lydia, remembering Jack Glover's remarks, looked closely at the chauffeur, and was startled to see a resemblance between him and the man who had driven the taxicab on the night she had been carried off from the theatre. It is true that the taxi driver had a moustache and that this man was clean-shaven, and moreover, had tiny side whiskers, but there was a resemblance.

"Have you had your driver long?" she asked as they were running through Monte Carlo, along the sea road.

"Mordon? Yes, we have had him six or seven years," said Jean carelessly. "He drives us when we are on the Continent, you know. He speaks French perfectly and is an excellent driver. Father has tried to persuade him to come to England, but he hates London – he was telling me the other day that he hadn't been there for ten years."

That disposed of the resemblance, thought Lydia, and yet – she could remember his voice, she thought, and when they alighted on the Promenade des Anglais she spoke to him. He replied in French, and it is impossible to detect points of resemblance in a voice that speaks one language and the same voice when it speaks another.

The promenade was crowded with saunterers. A band was playing by the jetty and although the wind was colder than it had been at Cap Martin the sun was warm enough to necessitate the opening of a parasol.

It was a race week, and the two girls lunched at the Negrito. They were in the midst of their meal when a man came toward them and Lydia recognised Mr Marcus Stepney. This dark, suave man was no favourite of hers, though why she could not have explained. His manners were always perfect and, towards her, deferential.

As usual, he was dressed with the precision of a fashion plate. Mr Marcus Stepney was a man, a considerable portion of whose time was taken up every morning by the choice of cravats and socks and shirts. Though Lydia did not know this, his smartness, plus a certain dexterity with cards, was his stock in trade. No breath of scandal had touched him, he moved in a good set and was always at the right place at the proper season.

When Aix was full he was certain to be found at the Palace, in the Deauville week you would find him at the Casino punting mildly at the baccarat table. And after the rooms were closed, and even the Sports Club at Monte Carlo had shut its doors, there was always a little game to be had in the hotels and in Marcus Stepney's private sitting-room.

And it cannot be denied that Mr Stepney was lucky. He won sufficient at these out-of-hour games to support him nobly through the trials and vicissitudes which the public tables inflict upon their votaries.

"Going to the races," he said, "how very fortunate! Will you come along with me? I can give you three good winners."

"I have no money to gamble," said Jean, "I am a poor woman. Lydia, who is rolling in wealth, can afford to take your tips, Marcus."

Marcus looked at Lydia with a speculative eye.

"If you haven't any money with you, don't worry. I have plenty and you can pay me afterwards. I could make you a million francs today."

"Thank you," said Jean coolly, "but Mrs Meredith does not bet so heavily."

Her tone was a clear intimation to the man of wits that he was impinging upon somebody else's preserves and he grinned amiably.

Nevertheless, it was a profitable afternoon for Lydia. She came back to Cap Martin twenty thousand francs richer than she had been when she started off.

"Lydia's had a lot of luck she tells me," said Mr Briggerland.

"Yes. She won about five hundred pounds," said his daughter. "Marcus was laying ground bait. She did not know what horses he had backed until after the race was run, when he invariably appeared with a few *mille* notes and Lydia's pleasure was pathetic. Of course she didn't win anything. The twenty thousand francs was a sprat – he's coming tonight to see how the whales are blowing!"

Mr Marcus Stepney arrived punctually, and, to Mr Briggerland's disgust, was dressed for dinner, a fact which necessitated the older man's hurried retreat and reappearance in conventional evening wear.

Marcus Stepney's behaviour at dinner was faultless. He devoted himself in the main to Mrs Cole-Mortimer and Jean, who apparently never looked at him and yet observed his every movement, knew that he was merely waiting his opportunity.

It came when the dinner was over and the party adjourned to the big stoep facing the sea. The night was chilly and Mr Stepney found wraps and furs for the ladies, and so manoeuvred the arrangement of the chairs that Lydia and he were detached from the remainder of the party, not by any great distance, but sufficient, as the experienced Marcus knew, to remove a murmured conversation from the sharpest eavesdropper.

Jean, who was carrying on a three-cornered conversation with her father and Mrs Cole-Mortimer, did not stir, until she saw, by the light of a shaded lamp in the roof, the dark head of Mr Marcus Stepney droop more confidently towards his companion. Then she rose and strolled across.

Marcus did not curse her because he did not express his inmost thoughts aloud.

He gave her his chair and pulled another forward.

"Does Miss Briggerland know?" asked Lydia.

"No," said Mr Stepney pleasantly.

"May I tell her?"

"Of course."

"Mr Stepney has been telling me about a wonderful racing coup to be made tomorrow. Isn't it rather thrilling, Jean? He says it will be quite possible for me to make five million francs without any risk at all."

"Except the risk of a million, I suppose," smiled Jean. "Well, are you going to do it?"

Lydia shook her head.

"I haven't a million francs in France, for one thing," she said, "and I wouldn't risk it if I had."

And Jean smiled again at the discomfiture which Mr Marcus Stepney strove manfully to hide.

Later she took his arm and led him into the garden.

"Marcus," she said when they were out of range of the house, "I think you are several kinds of a fool."

"Why?" asked the other, who was not in the best humour.

"It was so crude," she said scornfully, "so cheap and confidence-trickish. A miserable million francs – twenty thousand pounds. Apart from the fact that your name would be mud in London if it were known that you had robbed a girl – "

"There's no question of robbery," he said hotly, "I tell you Valdau is a certainty for the Prix."

"It would not be a certainty if her money were on," said Jean dryly. "It would finish an artistic second and you would be full of apologies, and poor Lydia would be a million francs to the bad. No, Marcus, that is cheap."

"I'm nearly broke," he said shortly.

He made no disguise of his profession, nor of his nefarious plan.

Between the two there was a queer kind of camaraderie. Though he may not have been privy to the more tremendous of her crimes, yet he seemed to accept her as one of those who lived on the frontiers of illegality.

"I was thinking about you, as you sat there telling her the story," said Jean thoughtfully. "Marcus, why don't you marry her?"

He stopped in his stride and looked down at the girl.

"Marry her, Jean; are you mad? She wouldn't marry me."

"Why not?" she asked. "Of course she'd marry you, you silly fool, if you went the right way about it."

He was silent.

"She is worth six hundred thousand pounds, and I happen to know that she has nearly two hundred thousand pounds in cash on deposit at the bank," said Jean.

"Why do you want me to marry her?" he asked significantly. "Is there a rake-off for you?"

"A big rake-off," she said. "The two hundred thousand on deposit should be easily get-at-able, Marcus, and she'd even give you more – "

"Why?" he asked.

"To agree to a separation," she said coolly. "I know you. No woman could live very long with you and preserve her reason."

He chuckled.

"And I'm to hand it all over to you?"

"Oh no," she corrected. "I'm not greedy. It is my experience that the greedy people get into bad trouble. The man or woman who 'wants it all' usually gets the dressing case the 'all' was kept in. No, I'd like to take a half."

He sat down on a garden seat and she followed his example.

"What is there to be?" he asked. "An agreement between you and me? Something signed and sealed and delivered, eh?" ∻

Her sad eyes caught his and held them.

"I trust you, Marcus," she said softly. "If I help you in this – and I will if you will do all that I tell you to do – I will trust you to give me my share."

Mr Marcus Stepney fingered his collar a little importantly.

"I've never let a pal down in my life," he said with a cough. "I'm as straight as they make 'em, to people who play the game with me."

"And you are wise, so far as I am concerned," said the gentle Jean. "For if you double-crossed me, I should hand the police the name and address of your other wife who is still living."

His jaw dropped.

"Wha – what?" he stammered.

"Let us join the ladies," mocked Jean, as she rose and put her arm in his.

It pleased her immensely to feel this big man trembling.

21

It seemed to Lydia that she had been abroad for years, though in reality she had been three days in Cap Martin, when Mr Marcus Stepney became a regular caller.

Even the most objectionable people improve on acquaintance, and give the lie to first impressions.

Mr Stepney never bored her. He had an inexhaustible store of anecdotes and reminiscences, none of which was in the slightest degree offensive. He was something of a sportsman, too, and he called by arrangement the next morning, after his introduction to the Cap Martin household, and conducting her to a sheltered cove, containing two bathing huts, he introduced her to the exhilarating Mediterranean.

Sea bathing is not permitted in Monte Carlo until May, and the water was much colder than Lydia had expected. They swam out to a floating platform when Mr Briggerland and Jean put in an appearance. Jean had come straight from the house in her bathing gown, over which she wore a light wrap. Lydia watched her with amazement, for the girl was an expert swimmer. She could dive from almost any height and could remain under water an alarming time.

"I never thought you had so much energy and strength in your little body," said Lydia, as Jean, with a shriek of enjoyment, drew herself on the raft and wiped the water from her eyes.

"There's a man up there looking at us through glasses," said Briggerland suddenly. "I saw the flash of the sun on them."

He pointed to the rising ground beyond the seashore, but they could see nothing.

Presently there was a glitter of light amongst the green, and Lydia pointed.

"I thought that sort of thing was never done except in comic newspapers," she said, but Jean did not smile. Her eyes were focused on the point where the unseen observer lay or sat, and she shaded her eyes.

"Some visitor from Monte Carlo, I expect. People at Cap Martin are much too respectable to do anything so vulgar."

Mr Briggerland, at a glance from his daughter, slipped into the water, and with strong heavy strokes, made his way to the shore.

"Father is going to investigate," said Jean, "and the water really is the warmest place," and with that she fell sideways into the blue sea like a seal, dived down into its depths, and presently Lydia saw her walking along the white floor of the ocean, her little hands keeping up an almost imperceptible motion. Presently she shot up again, shook her head and looked round, only to dive again.

In the meantime, though Lydia, who was fascinated by the manoeuvre of the girl, did not notice the fact, Mr Briggerland had reached the shore, pulled on a pair of rubber shoes, and with his mackintosh buttoned over his bathing dress had begun to climb through the underbrush towards the spot where the glasses had glistened. When Lydia looked up he had disappeared.

"Where is your father?" she asked the girl.

"He went into the bushes." Mr Stepney volunteered the information. "I suppose he's looking for the Paul Pry."

Mr Stepney had been unusually glum and silent, for he was piqued by the tactless appearance of the Briggerlands.

"Come into the water, Marcus," said Jean peremptorily, as she put her foot against the edge of the raft, and pushed herself backward, "I want to see Mrs Meredith dive."

"Me?" said Lydia in surprise. "Good heavens, no! After watching you I don't intend making an exhibition of myself."

"I want to show you the proper way to dive," said Jean. "Stand up on the edge of the raft."

Lydia obeyed.

"Straight up," said Jean. "Now put both your arms out wide. Now – "

There was a sharp crack from the shore; something whistled past Lydia's head, struck an upright post, splintering the edge, and with a whine went ricochetting into the sea.

Lydia's face went white.

"What – what was that?" she gasped. She had hardly spoken before there was another shot. This time the bullet must have gone very high, and immediately afterwards came a yell of pain from the shore.

Jean did not wait. She struck out for the beach, swimming furiously. It was not the shot, but the cry which had alarmed her, and without waiting to put on coat or sandals, she ran up the little road where her father had gone, following the path through the undergrowth. Presently she came to a grassy plot, in the centre of which two tall pines grew side by side, and lying against one of the trees was the huddled figure of Briggerland. She turned him over. He was breathing heavily and was unconscious. An ugly wound gaped at the back of his head, and his mackintosh and bathing dress were smothered with blood.

She looked round quickly for his assailant, but there was nobody in sight, and nothing to indicate the presence of a third person but two shining brass cartridges which lay on the grass.

22

Lydia Meredith only remembered swooning twice in her life, and both these occasions had happened within a few weeks.

She never felt quite so unprepared to carry on as she did when, with an effort, she threw herself into the water at Marcus Stepney's side and swam slowly toward the shore.

She dare not let her mind dwell upon the narrowness of her escape. Whoever had fired that shot had done so deliberately, and with the intention of killing her. She had felt the wind of the bullet in her face.

"What do you suppose it was?" asked Marcus Stepney as he assisted her up the beach. "Do you think it was soldiers practising?"

She shook her head.

"Oh," said Mr Stepney thoughtfully, and then: "If you don't mind, I'll run up and see what has happened."

He wrapped himself in the dressing gown he had brought with him, and followed Jean's trail, coming up with her as Mr Briggerland opened his eyes and stared round.

"Help me to hold him, Marcus," said Jean. "Wait a moment," said Mr Stepney, feeling in his pocket and producing a silk handkerchief, "bandage him with that."

She shook her head.

"He's lost all the blood he's going to lose," she said quietly, "and I don't think there's a fracture. I felt the skull very carefully with my finger."

Mr Stepney shivered.

"Hullo," said Briggerland drowsily, "Gee, he gave me a whack!"

"Who did it?" asked the girl.

Mr Briggerland shook his head and winced with the pain of it.

"I don't know," he moaned. "Help me up, Stepney."

With the man's assistance he rose unsteadily to his feet.

"What happened?" asked Stepney.

"Don't ask him any questions now," said the girl sharply. "Help him back to the house."

A doctor was summoned and stitched the wound. He gave an encouraging report, and was not too inquisitive as to how the injury had occurred. Foreign visitors get extraordinary things in the regions of Monte Carlo, and medical men lose nothing by their discretion.

It was not until that afternoon, propped up with pillows in a chair, the centre of a sympathetic audience, that Mr Briggerland told his story.

"I had a feeling that something was wrong," he said, "and I went up to investigate. I heard a shot fired, almost within a few yards of me, and dashing through the bushes I saw the fellow taking aim for the second time, and seized him. You remember the second shot went high."

"What sort of a man was he?" asked Stepney.

"He was an Italian, I should think," answered Mr Briggerland. "At any rate, he caught me an awful whack with the back of his rifle, and I knew no more until Jean found me."

"Do you think he was firing at me?" asked Lydia in horror.

"I am certain of it," said Briggerland.

"I realised it the moment I saw the fellow."

"How am I to thank you?" said the girl impulsively. "Really, it was wonderful of you to tackle an armed man with your bare hands."

Mr Briggerland closed his eyes and sighed.

"It was nothing," he said modestly.

Before dinner he and his daughter were left alone for the first time since the accident.

"What happened?" she asked.

"It was going to be a little surprise for you," he said. "A little scheme of my own, my dear; you're always calling me a funk, and I wanted to prove – "

"What happened?" she asked tersely.

"Well, I went out yesterday morning and fixed it all. I bought the rifle, an old English rifle, at Amiens from a peasant. I thought it might come in handy, especially as the man threw in a packet of ammunition. Yesterday morning, lying awake before daybreak, I thought it out. I went up to the hill – the land belongs to an empty house, by the way – and I located the spot, put the rifle where I could find it easily, and fixed a pair of glass goggles on to one of the bushes, where the sun would catch it. The whole scheme was not without its merit as a piece of strategy, my dear," he said complacently.

"And then – ?" she said.

"I thought we'd go bathing yesterday, but we didn't, but today – it was a long time before anybody spotted the glasses, but once I had the excuse for going ashore and investigating, the rest was easy."

She nodded.

"So that was why you asked me to keep her on the raft, and make her stand up?"

He nodded.

"Well – ?" she demanded.

"I went up to the spot, got the rifle and took aim. I've always been a pretty good shot – "

"You didn't advertise it today," she said sardonically. "Then I suppose somebody hit you on the head?"

He nodded and made a grimace, but any movement of his injured cranium was excessively painful.

"Who was it?" she asked.

He shrugged his shoulders.

"Don't ask fool questions," he said petulantly. "I know nothing. I didn't even feel the blow. I just remember taking aim, and then everything went dark."

"And how would you have explained it all, supposing you had succeeded?"

"That was easy," he said. "I should have said that I went in search of the man we had seen, I heard a shot and rushed forward and found nothing but the rifle."

She was silent, pinching her lips absently. "And you took the risk of some peasant or visitor seeing you – took the risk of bringing the police to the spot and turning what might have easily been a case of accidental death into an obvious case of wilful murder. I think you called yourself a strategist," she asked politely.

"I did my best," he growled.

"Well, don't do it again, father," she said. "Your foolhardiness appals me, and heaven knows, I never expected that I should be in a position to call you foolhardy."

And with this she left him to bask in the hero-worship which the approaching Mrs Cole-Mortimer would lavish upon him.

The "accident" kept them at home that night, and Lydia was not sorry. A settee is not a very comfortable sleeping place, and she was ready for a real bed that night. Mr Stepney found her yawning surreptitiously, and went home early in disgust.

The night was warmer than the morning had been. The *Föhn* wind was blowing and she found her room with its radiator a little oppressive. She opened the long French windows, and stepped out on to the balcony. The last quarter of the moon was high in the sky, and though the light was faint, it gave shadows to trees and an eerie illumination to the lawn.

She leant her arms on the rail and looked across the sea to the lights of Monte Carlo glistening in the purple night. Her eyes wandered idly to the grounds and she started. She could have sworn she had seen a figure moving in the shadow of the tree, nor was she mistaken.

Presently it left the tree belt, and stepped cautiously across the lawn, halting now and again to look around. She thought at first that it was Marcus Stepney who had returned, but something about the walk of the man seemed familiar. Presently he stopped directly under the balcony and looked up and she uttered an exclamation, as the faint light revealed the iron-grey hair and the grisly eyebrows of the intruder.

"All right, miss," he said in a hoarse whisper, "it's only old Jaggs."

"What are you doing?" she answered in the same tone.

"Just lookin' round," he said, "just lookin' round," and limped again into the darkness.

23

So old Jaggs was in Monte Carlo! Whatever was he doing, and how was he getting on with these people who spoke nothing but French, she wondered! She had something to think about before she went to sleep.

She opened her eyes singularly awake as the dawn was coming up over the grey sea. She looked at her watch; it was a quarter to six. Why she had wakened so thoroughly she could not tell, but remembered with a little shiver another occasion she had wakened, this time before the dawn, to face death in a most terrifying shape.

She got up out of bed, put on a heavy coat and opened the wire doors that led to the balcony. The morning was colder than she imagined, and she was glad to retreat to the neighbourhood of the warm radiator.

The fresh clean hours of the dawn, when the mind is clear, and there is neither sound nor movement to distract the thoughts, are favourable to sane thinking.

Lydia reviewed the past few weeks in her life, and realised, for the first time, the miracle which had happened. It was like a legend of old – the slave had been lifted from the king's ante-room – the struggling artist was now a rich woman. She twiddled the gold ring on her hand absent-mindedly – and she was married…and a widow! She had an uncomfortable feeling that, in spite of her riches, she had not yet found her niche. She was an odd quantity, as yet. The Cole-Mortimers and the Briggerlands did not belong to her ideal world, and she could find no place where she fitted.

She tried, in this state of mind so favourable to the consideration of such a problem, to analyse Jack Glover's antagonism toward Jean Briggerland and her father.

It seemed unnatural that a healthy young man should maintain so bitter a feud with a girl whose beauty was almost of a transcendant quality and all because she had rejected him.

Jack Glover was a public schoolboy, a man with a keen sense of honour. She could not imagine him being guilty of a mean action. And such men did not pursue vendettas without good reason. If they were rejected by a woman, they accepted their congé, with a good grace, and it was almost unthinkable that Jack should have no other reason for his hatred. Yet she could not bring herself even to consider the possibility that the reason was the one he had advanced. She came again to the dead end of conjecture. She could believe in Jack's judgment up to a point – beyond that she could not go.

She had her bath, dressed, and was in the garden when the eastern horizon was golden with the light of the rising sun. Nobody was about, the most energetic of the servants had not yet risen, and she strolled through the avenue to the main road. As she stood there looking up and down a man came out from the trees that fringed the road and began walking rapidly in the direction of Monte Carlo.

"Mr Jaggs!" she called.

He took no notice, but seemed to increase his limping pace, and after a moment's hesitation, she went flying down the road after him. He turned at the sound of her footsteps and in his furtive way drew into the shadow of a bush. He looked more than usually grimy; on his hands were an odd pair of gloves and a soft slouch hat, that had seen better days, covered his head.

"Good morning, miss," he wheezed.

"Why were you running away, Mr Jaggs?" she asked, a little out of breath.

"Not runnin' away, miss," he said, glancing at her sharply from under his heavy white eyebrows. "Just havin' a look round!"

"Do you spend all your nights looking round?" she smiled at him.

"Yes, miss."

At that moment a cyclist gendarme came into view. He slowed down as he approached the two and dismounted.

"Good morning, madame," he said politely, and then looking at the man, "is this man in your employ? I have seen him coming out of your house every morning?"

"Oh, yes," said Lydia hastily, "he's my – "

She was at a loss to describe him, but old Jaggs saved her the trouble.

"I'm madame's courier," he said, and to Lydia's amazement he spoke in perfect French, "I am also the watchman of the house."

"Yes, yes," said Lydia, after she had recovered from her surprise. "M'sieur is the watchman, also."

"*Bien*, madame," said the gendarme. "Forgive my asking, but we have so many strangers here."

They watched the gendarme out of sight. Then old Jaggs chuckled.

"Pretty good French, miss, wasn't it?" he said, and without another word turned and limped in the trail of the police.

She looked after him in bewilderment. So he spent every night in the grounds, or somewhere about the house? The knowledge gave her a queer sense of comfort and safety.

When she went back to the villa she found the servants were up. Jean did not put in an appearance until breakfast, and Lydia had an opportunity of talking to the French housekeeper whom Mrs Cole-Mortimer had engaged when she took the villa. From her she learnt a bit of news, which she passed on to Jean almost as soon as she put in an appearance.

"The gardener's little boy is going to get well, Jean."

Jean nodded.

"I know," she said. "I telephoned to the hospital yesterday."

It was so unlike her conception of the girl, that Lydia stared.

"The mother is in isolation," Lydia went on, "and Madame Souviet says that the poor woman has no money and no friends. I thought of going down to the hospital today to see if I could do anything for her."

"You'd better not, my dear," warned Mrs Cole-Mortimer nervously. "Let us be thankful we've got the little brat out of the neighbourhood without our catching the disease. One doesn't want to seek trouble. Keep away from the hospital."

"Rubbish!" said Jean briskly. "If Lydia wants to go, there is no reason why she shouldn't. The isolation people are never allowed to come into contact with visitors, so there is really no danger."

"I agree with Mrs Cole-Mortimer," grumbled Briggerland. "It is very foolish to ask for trouble. You take my advice, my dear, and keep away."

"I had a talk with a gendarme this morning," said Lydia to change the subject. "When he stopped and got off his bicycle I thought he was going to speak about the shooting. I suppose it was reported to the police?"

"Er – yes," said Mr Briggerland, not looking up from his plate, "of course. Have you been into Monte Carlo?"

Lydia shook her head.

"No, I couldn't sleep, and I was taking a walk along the road when he passed." She said nothing about Mr Jaggs. "The police at Monaco are very sociable."

Mr Briggerland sniffed.

"Very," he said.

"Have they any theories?" she asked. In her innocence she was persisting in a subject which was wholly distasteful to Mr Briggerland. "About the shooting I mean?"

"Yes, they have theories, but my dear, I should advise you not to discuss the matter with the police. The fact is," invented Mr Briggerland, "I told them that you were unaware of the fact that you had been shot at, and if you discussed it with the police, you would make me look rather foolish."

When Lydia and Mrs Cole-Mortimer had gone, Jean seized an opportunity which the absence of the maid offered.

"I hope you are beginning to see how perfectly insane your scheme was," she said. "You have to support your act with a whole series of bungling lies. Possibly Marcus, like a fool, has mentioned it in

115

Monte Carlo, and we shall have the detectives out here asking why you have not reported the matter."

"If I were as clever as you – " he growled.

"You're not," said Jean, rolling her serviette. "You're the most un-clever man I know."

24

Lydia went up to her bedroom to put away her clothes and found the maid making the bed.

"Oh, madame," said the girl, "I forgot to speak to you about a matter – I hope madame will not be angry."

"I'm hardly likely to be angry on a morning like this," said Lydia.

"It is because of this matter," said the girl. She groped in her pocket and brought out a small shining object, and Lydia took it from her hand.

"This matter" was a tiny silver cross, so small that a five-franc piece would have covered it easily. It was brightly polished and apparently had seen service.

"When we took your bed, after the atrocious and mysterious happening," said the maid rapidly, "this was found in the sheets. It was not thought that it could possibly be madame's, because it was so poor, until this morning when it was suggested that it might be a souvenir that madame values."

"You found it in the sheets?" asked Lydia in surprise.

"Yes, madame."

"It doesn't belong to me," said Lydia. "Perhaps it belongs to Madame Cole-Mortimer. I will show it to her."

Mrs Cole-Mortimer was a devout Catholic and it might easily be some cherished keepsake of hers.

The girl carried the cross to the window; an "X" had been scrawled by some sharp-pointed instrument at the junction of the bars. There was no other mark to identify the trinket.

She put the cross in her bag, and when she saw Mrs Cole-Mortimer again she forgot to ask her about it.

The car drove her into Nice alone. Jean did not feel inclined to make the journey and Lydia rather enjoyed the solitude.

The isolation hospital was at the top of the hill and she found some difficulty in obtaining admission at this hour. The arrival of the chief medical officer, however, saved her from making the journey in vain. The report he gave about the child was very satisfactory; the mother was in the isolation ward.

"Can she be seen?"

"Yes, madame," said the urbane Frenchman in charge. "You understand, you will not be able to get near her? It will be rather like interviewing a prisoner, for she will be behind one set of bars and you behind another."

Lydia was taken to a room which was, she imagined, very much like a room in which prisoners interviewed their distressed relations. There were not exactly bars, but two large mesh nets of steel separated the visitor from the patient under observation. After a time a nun brought in the gardener's wife, a tall, gaunt woman, who was a native of Marseilles, and spoke the confusing patois of that city with great rapidity. It was some time before Lydia could accustom her ear to the queer dialect.

Her boy was getting well, she said, but she herself was in terrible trouble. She had no money for the extra food she required. Her husband, who was away in Paris when the child had been taken, had not troubled to write to her. It was terrible being in a place amongst other fever cases, and she was certain that her days were numbered…

Lydia pushed a five-hundred franc note through the grating to the nun, to settle her material needs.

"And, oh, madame," wailed the gardener's wife, "my poor little boy has lost the gift of the Reverend Mother of San Surplice! His own cross which has been blessed by his holiness the Pope! It is because I left his cross in his little shirt that he is getting better, but now it is lost and I am sure these thieving doctors have taken it."

"A cross?" said Lydia. "What sort of a cross?"

"It was a silver cross, madame; the value in money was nothing – it was priceless. Little Xavier – "

"Xavier?" repeated Lydia, remembering the "X" on the trinket that had been found in her bed. "Wait a moment, madame." She opened her bag and took out the tiny silver symbol, and at the sight of it the woman burst into a volley of joyful thanks.

"It is the same, the same, madame! It has a small 'X' which the Reverend Mother scratched with her own blessed scissors!"

Lydia pushed the cross through the net and the nun handed it to the woman.

"It is the same, it is the same!" she cried.

"Oh, thank you, madame! Now my heart is glad…"

Lydia came out of the hospital and walked through the gardens by the doctor's side. But she was not listening to what he was saying – her mind was fully occupied with the mystery of the silver cross.

It was little Xavier's…it had been tucked inside his bed when he lay, as his mother thought, dying…and it had been found in her bed! Then little Xavier had been in her bed! Her foot was on the step of the car when it came to her – the meaning of that drenched couch and the empty bottle of peroxide. Xavier had been put there, and somebody who knew that the bed was infected had so soaked it with water that she could not sleep in it. But who? Old Jaggs!

She got into the car slowly, and went back to Cap Martin along the Grande Corniche.

Who had put the child there? He could not have walked from the cottage; that was impossible.

She was halfway home when she noticed a parcel lying on the floor of the car, and she let down the front window and spoke to the chauffeur. It was not Mordon, but a man whom she had hired with the car.

"It came from the hospital, madame," he said. "The porter asked me if I came from Villa Casa. It was something sent to the hospital to be disinfected. There was a charge of seven francs for the service, madame, and this I paid."

She nodded.

She picked up the parcel – it was addressed to "Mademoiselle Jean Briggerland" and bore the label of the hospital.

Lydia sat back in the car with her eyes closed, tired of turning over this problem, yet determined to get to the bottom of the mystery.

Jean was out when she got back and she carried the parcel to her own room. She was trying to keep out of her mind the very possibility that such a hideous crime could have been conceived as that which all the evidence indicated had been attempted. Very resolutely she refused to believe that such a thing could have happened. There must be some explanation for the presence of the cross in her bed. Possibly it had been found after the wet sheets had been taken to the servants' part of the house.

She rang the bell, and the maid who had given her the trinket came.

"Tell me," said Lydia, "where was this cross found?"

"In your bed, mademoiselle."

"But where? Was it before the clothing was removed from this room or after?"

"It was before, madame," said the maid. "When the sheets were turned back we found it lying exactly in the middle of the bed."

Lydia's heart sank.

"Thank you, that will do," she said. "I have found the owner of the cross and have restored it."

Should she tell Jean? Her first impulse was to take the girl into her confidence, and reveal the state of her mind. Her second thought was to seek out old Jaggs, but where could he be found? He evidently lived somewhere in Monte Carlo, but his name was hardly likely to be in the visitors' list. She was still undecided when Marcus Stepney called to take her to lunch at the Café de Paris.

The whole thing was so amazingly improbable. It belonged to a world of unreality, but then, she told herself, she also was living in an unreal world, and had been so for weeks.

25

Mr Stepney had become more bearable. A week ago she would have shrunk from taking luncheon with him, but now such a prospect had no terrors. His views of things and people were more generous than she had expected. She had anticipated his attitude would be a little cynical, but to her surprise he oozed loving kindness. Had she known Mr Marcus Stepney as well as Joan knew him, she would have realised that he adapted his mental attitude to his audience. He was a man whose stock-in-trade was a knowledge of human nature, and the ability to please. He would no more have attempted to shock or frighten her, than a first-class salesman would shock or annoy a possible customer.

He had goods to sell, and it was his business to see that they satisfied the buyer. In this case the goods were represented by sixty-nine inches of good-looking, well-dressed man, and it was rather important that he should present the best face of the article to the purchaser. It was almost as important that the sale should be a quick one. Mr Stepney lived from week to week. What might happen next year seldom interested him, therefore his courting must be rapid.

He told the story of his life at lunch, a story liable to move a tender-hearted woman to at least a sympathetic interest. The story of his life varied also with the audience. In this case, it was designed for one whom he knew had had a hard struggle, whose father had been heavily in debt, and who had tasted some of the bitterness of defeat. Jean had given him a very precise story of the girl's career, and Mr Marcus Stepney adapted it for his own purpose.

"Why, your life has almost run parallel with mine," said Lydia.

"I hope it may continue," said Mr Stepney not without a touch of sadness in his voice. "I am a very lonely man – I have no friends except the acquaintances one can pick up at night clubs, and the places where the smart people go in the season, and there is an artificiality about society friends which rather depresses me."

"I feel that, too," said the sympathetic Lydia.

"If I could only settle down!" he said, shaking his head. "A little house in the country, a few horses, a few cows, a woman who understood me…"

A false move this.

"And a few pet chickens to follow you about?" she laughed. "No, it doesn't sound quite like you, Mr Stepney."

He lowered his eyes.

"I am sorry you think that," he said. "All the world thinks that I'm a gadabout, an idler, with no interest in existence, except the pleasure I can extract."

"And a jolly good existence, too," said Lydia briskly. She had detected a note of sentiment creeping into the conversation, and had slain it with the most effective weapon in woman's armoury.

"And now tell me all about the great Moorish Pretender who is staying at your hotel – I caught a glimpse of him on the promenade – and there was a lot about him in the paper."

Mr Stepney sighed and related all that he knew of the redoubtable Muley Hafiz on the way to the rooms. Muley Hafiz was being lionised in France just then, to the annoyance of the Spanish authorities, who had put a price on his head.

Lydia showed much more interest in the Moorish Pretender than she did in the pretender who walked by her side.

He was not in the best of tempers when he brought her back to the Villa Casa, and Jean, who entertained him whilst Lydia was changing, saw that his first advances had not met with a very encouraging result.

"There will be no wedding bells, Jean," he said.

"You take a rebuff very easily," said the girl, but he shook his head.

"My dear Jean, I know women as well as I know the back of my hand, and I tell you that there's nothing doing with this girl. I'm not a fool."

She looked at him earnestly.

"No, you're not a fool," she said at last. "You're hardly likely to make a mistake about that sort of thing. I'm afraid you'll have to do something more romantic."

"What do you mean?" he asked.

"You'll have to run away with her; and like the knights of old carry off the lady of your choice."

"The knights of old didn't have to go before a judge and jury and serve seven years at Dartmoor for their sins," he said unpleasantly.

She was sitting on a low chair overlooking the sea, whittling a twig with a silver-handled knife she had taken from her bag — a favourite occupation of hers in moments of cogitation.

"All the ladies of old didn't go to the police," she said. "Some of them were quite happy with their powerful lords, especially delicate-minded ladies who shrank from advertising their misfortune to the readers of the Sunday press. I think most women like to be wooed in the caveman fashion, Marcus."

"Is that the kind of treatment you'd like, Jean?"

There was a new note in his voice. Had she looked at him she would have seen a strange light in his eyes.

"I'm merely advancing a theory," she said, "a theory which has been supported throughout the ages."

"I'd let her go and her money, too," he said. He was speaking quickly, almost incoherently. "There's only one woman in the world for me, Jean, and I've told you that before. I'd give my life and soul for her."

He bent over, and caught her arm in his big hand.

"You believe in the caveman method, do you?" he breathed. "It is the kind of treatment you'd like, eh, Jean?"

She did not attempt to release her arm.

"Keep your hand to yourself, Marcus, please," she said quietly.

"You'd like it, wouldn't you, Jean? My God, I'd sacrifice my soul for you, you little devil!"

"Be sensible," she said. It was not her words or her firm tone that made him draw back. Twice and deliberately she drew the edge of her little knife across the back of his hand, and he leapt away with a howl of pain.

"You — you beast," he stammered, and she looked at him with her sly smile.

"There must have been cavewomen, too, Marcus," she said coolly, as she rose. "They had their methods — give me your handkerchief, I want to wipe this knife."

His face was grey now. He was looking at her like a man bereft of his senses.

He did not move when she took his handkerchief from his pocket, wiped the knife, closed and slipped it into her bag, before she replaced the handkerchief tidily. And all the time he stood there with his hand streaming with blood, incapable of movement. It was not until she had disappeared round the corner of the house that he pulled out the handkerchief and wrapped it about his hand.

"A devil," he whimpered, almost in tears, "a devil!"

26

Jean Briggerland discovered a new arrival on her return to the house.

Jack Glover had come unexpectedly from London, so Lydia told her, and Jack himself met her with extraordinary geniality.

"You lucky people to be in this paradise!" he said. "It is raining like the dickens in London, and miserable beyond description. And you're looking brown and beautiful, Miss Briggerland."

"The spirit of the warm south has got into your blood, Mr Glover," she said sarcastically. "A course at the Riviera would make you almost human."

"And what would make you human?" asked Jack blandly.

"I hope you people aren't going to quarrel as soon as you meet," said Lydia.

Jean was struck by the change in the girl. There was a colour in her cheeks, and a new and a more joyous note in her voice, which was unmistakable to so keen a student as Jean Briggerland.

"I never quarrel with Jack," she said. She assumed a proprietorial air toward Jack Glover, which unaccountably annoyed Lydia. "He invents the quarrels and carries them out himself. How long are you staying?"

"Two days," said Jack, "then I'm due back in town."

"Have you brought your Mr Jaggs with you?" asked Jean innocently.

"Isn't he here?" asked Jack in surprise. "I sent him along a week ago."

"Here?" repeated Jean slowly. "Oh, he's here, is he? Of course." She nodded. Certain things were clear to her now; the unknown drencher of beds, the stranger who had appeared from nowhere and had left her father senseless, were no longer mysteries.

"Oh, Jean," it was Lydia who spoke. "I'm awfully remiss, I didn't give you the parcel I brought back from the hospital."

"From the hospital?" said Jean. "What parcel was that?"

"Something you had sent to be sterilized. I'll get it."

She came back in a minute or two with the parcel which she had found in the car.

"Oh yes," said Jean carelessly, "I remember. It is a rug that I lent to the gardener's wife when her little boy was taken ill."

She handed the packet to the maid.

"Take it to my room," she said.

She waited just long enough to find an excuse for leaving the party, and went upstairs. The parcel was on her bed. She tore off the wrapping – inside, starched white and clean, was the dust coat she had worn the night she had carried Xavier from the cottage to Lydia's bed. The rubber cap was there, discoloured from the effects of the disinfectant, and the gloves and the silk handkerchief, neatly washed and pressed. She looked at them thoughtfully.

She put the articles away in a drawer, went down the servants' stairs and through a heavy open door into the cellar. Light was admitted by two barred windows, through one of which she had thrust her bundle that night, and she could see every corner of the cellar, which was empty – as she had expected. The clothing she had thrown down had been gathered by some mysterious agent, who had forwarded it to the hospital in her name.

She came slowly up the stairs, fastened the open door behind her, and walked out into the garden to think.

"Jaggs!" she said aloud, and her voice was as soft as silk. "I think, Mr Jaggs, you ought to be in heaven."

27

"Who were the haughty individuals interviewing Jean in the saloon?" asked Jack Glover, as Lydia's car panted and groaned on the stiff ascent to La Turbie.

Lydia was concerned, and he had already noted her seriousness.

"Poor Jean is rather worried," she said. "It appears that she had a love affair with a man three or four years ago, and recently he has been bombarding her with threatening letters."

"Poor soul," said Jack dryly. "but I should imagine she could have dealt with that matter without calling in the police. I suppose they were detectives. Has she had a letter recently?"

"She had one this morning – posted in Monte Carlo last night."

"By the way, Jean went into Monte Carlo last night, didn't she?" asked Jack.

She looked at him reproachfully.

"We all went into Monte Carlo," she said severely. "Now, please don't be horrid, Mr Glover, you aren't suggesting that Jean wrote this awful letter to herself, are you?"

"Was it an awful letter?" asked Jack.

"A terrible letter, threatening to kill her. Do you know that Mr Briggerland thinks that the person who nearly killed me was really shooting at Jean."

"You don't say," said Jack politely. "I haven't heard about people shooting at you – but it sounds rather alarming."

She told him the story, and he offered no comment.

"Go on with your thrilling story of Jean's mortal enemy. Who is he?"

"She doesn't know his name," said Lydia. "She met him in Egypt – an elderly man who positively dogged her footsteps wherever she went, and made himself a nuisance."

"Doesn't know his name, eh?" said Jack with a sniff. "Well, that's convenient."

"I think you're almost spiteful," said Lydia hotly. "Poor girl, she was so distressed this morning; I have never seen her so upset."

"And are the police going to keep guard and follow her wherever she goes? And is that impossible person, Mr Marcus Stepney, also in the vendetta? I saw him wandering about this morning like a wounded hero, with his arm in a sling."

"He hurt his hand gathering wild flowers for me on the – "

But Jack's outburst of laughter checked her, and she glared at him.

"I think you're boorish," she snapped angrily. "I'm sorry I came out with you."

"And I'm sorry I've been such a fool," apologised the penitent Jack, "but the vision of the immaculate Mr Stepney gathering wild flowers in a top hat and a morning suit certainly did appeal to me as being comical!"

"He doesn't wear a top hat or a morning suit in Monte Carlo," she said, furious at his banter. "Let us talk about somebody else than my friends."

"I haven't started to talk about your friends yet," he said. "And please don't try to tell your chauffeur to turn round – the road is too narrow, and he'd have the car over the cliff before you knew where you were, if he were stupid enough to try. I'm sorry, deeply sorry, Mrs Meredith, but I think that Jean was right when she said that the southern air had got into my blood. I'm a little hysterical – yes, put it down to that. It runs in the family," he babbled on. "I have an aunt who faints at the sight of strawberries, and an uncle who swoons whenever a cat walks into the room."

"I hope you don't visit him very much," she said coldly.

"Two points to you," said Jack, "but I must warn Jaggs, in case he is mistaken for the elderly Lothario. Obviously Jean is preparing the way for an unpleasant end to poor old Jaggs."

"Why do you think these things about Jean?" she asked, as they were running into La Turbie.

"Because I have a criminal mind," he replied promptly. "I have the same type of mind as Jean Briggerland's, wedded to a wholesome respect for the law, and a healthy sense of right and wrong. Some people couldn't be happy if they owned a cent that had been earned dishonestly; other people are happy so long as they have the money – so long as it is real money. I belong to the former category. Jean – well, I don't know what would make Jean happy."

"And what would make you happy – Jean?" she asked.

He did not answer this question until they were sitting on the stoep of the National, where a light luncheon was awaiting them.

"Jean?" he said, as though the question had just been asked. "No, I don't want Jean. She is wonderful, really, Mrs Meredith, wonderful! I find myself thinking about her at odd moments, and the more I think the more I am amazed. Lucretia Borgia was a child in arms compared with Jean – poor old Lucretia has been maligned, anyway. There was a woman in the sixteenth century rather like her, and another girl in the early days of New England, who used to denounce witches for the pleasure of seeing them burn, but I can't think of an exact parallel, because Jean gets no pleasure out of hurting people any more than you will get out of cutting that cantaloup. It has just got to be cut, and the fact that you are finally destroying the life of the melon doesn't worry you."

"Have cantaloups life?" She paused, knife in hand, eyeing the fruit with a frown. "No, I don't think I want it. So Jean is a murderess at heart?"

She asked the question in solemn mockery, but Jack was not smiling.

"Oh yes – in intention, at any rate. I don't know whether she has ever killed anybody, but she has certainly planned murders."

Lydia sighed and sat back in her chair patiently.

"Do you still suggest that she harbours designs against my young life?"

"I not only suggest it, but I state positively that there have been four attempts on your life in the past fortnight," he said calmly.

"Let us have this out," she said recklessly. "Number one?"

"The nearly-a-fatal accident in Berkeley Street," said Jack.

"Will you explain by what miracle the car arrived at the psychological moment?" she asked.

"That's easy," he said with a smile. "Old man Briggerland lit his cigar standing on the steps of the house. That light was a brilliant one, Jaggs tells me. It was the signal for the car to come on. The next attempt was made with the assistance of a lunatic doctor who was helped to escape by Briggerland, and brought to your house by him. In some way he got hold of a key – probably Jean manoeuvred it. Did she ever talk to you about keys?"

"No," said the girl, "she – " She stopped suddenly, remembering that Jean had discussed keys with her.

"Are you sure she didn't?" asked Jack, watching her.

"I think she may have done," said the girl defiantly; "what was the third attempt?"

"The third attempt," said Jack slowly, "was to infect your bed with a malignant fever."

"Jean did it?" said the girl incredulously. "Oh no, that would be impossible."

"The child was in your bed. Jaggs saw it and threw two buckets of water over the bed, so that you should not sleep in it."

She was silent.

"And I suppose the next attempt was the shooting?"

He nodded.

"Now do you believe?" he asked.

She shook her head.

"No, I don't believe," she said quietly.

"I think you have worked up a very strong case against poor Jean, and I am sure you think you're justified."

"You are quite right there," he said.

He lifted a pair of field glasses which he had put on the table, and surveyed the road from the sea. "Mrs Meredith, I want you to do something and tell Jean Briggerland when you have done it."

"What is that?" she asked.

"I want you to make a will. I don't care where you leave your property, so long as it is not to somebody you love."

She shivered.

"I don't like making wills. It's so gruesome."

"It will be more gruesome for you if you don't," he said significantly. "The Briggerlands are your heirs at law."

She looked at him quickly.

"So that is what you are aiming at? You think that all these plots are designed to put me out of the way so that they can enjoy my money?"

He nodded, and she looked at him wonderingly.

"If you weren't a hard-headed lawyer, I should think you were a writer of romantic fiction," she said. "But if it will please you I will make a will. I haven't the slightest idea who I could leave the money to. I've got rather a lot of money, haven't I?"

"You have exactly £160,000 in hard cash. I want to talk to you about that," said Jack. "It is lying at your bankers in your current account. It represents property which has been sold or was in process of being sold when you inherited the money, and anybody who can get your signature and can satisfy the bankers that they are bona fide payees, can draw every cent you have of ready money. I might say in passing that we are prepared for that contingency, and any large cheque will be referred to me or to my partner."

He raised his field glasses for a second time and looked steadily down along the hill road up which they had come.

"Are you expecting anybody?" she asked.

"I'm expecting Jean," he said grimly.

"But we left her – "

"The fact that we left her talking to the police doesn't mean that she will not be coming up here, to watch us. Jean doesn't like me, you know, and she will be scared to death of this *tête-à-tête.*"

The conversation had been arrested by the arrival of the soup and now there was a further interruption whilst the table was being cleared. When the *maître d'hôtel* had gone the girl asked: "What am I to do with the money? Reinvest it?"

"Exactly," said Jack, "but the most important thing is to make your will."

He looked along the deserted veranda. They were the only guests present who had come early. From the veranda two curtained doors led into the *salon* of the hotel and it struck him that one of these had not been ajar when he looked at it before, and it was the door opposite to the table where they were sitting.

He noted this idly without attaching any great importance to the fact.

"Suppose somebody were to present a cheque to the bank in my name?" she asked. "What would happen?"

"If it were for a large sum? The manager would call us up and one of us would probably go round to your bank. It is only a block from our office. If Rennett or I said it was all right the cheque would be honoured. You may be sure that I should make very drastic inquiries as to the origin of the signature."

And then she saw him stiffen and his eyes go to the door. He waited a second, then rising noiselessly, crossed the wooden floor of the veranda quickly and pushed open the door, to find himself face to face with the smiling Jean Briggerland.

28

"However did you get here?" asked Lydia in surprise.

"I went into Nice," said the girl carelessly. "The detectives were going there and I gave them a lift."

"I see," said Jack, "so you came into Turbie by the back road? I wondered why I hadn't seen your car."

"You expected me, did you?" she smiled, as she sat down at the table and selected a peach from its cotton-wool bed. "I only arrived a second ago, in fact I was opening the door when you almost knocked my head off. What a violent man you are, Jack! I shall have to put you into my story."

Glover had recovered his self-possession by now.

"So you are adding to your other crimes by turning novelist, are you?" he said good-humouredly. "What is the book, Miss Briggerland?"

"It is going to be called 'Suspected'," she said coolly. "And it will be the Story of a Hurt Soul."

"Oh, I see, a humourous story," said Jack, wilfully dense. "I didn't know you were going to write a biography."

"But do tell me about this, it is very thrilling, Jean," said Lydia, "and it is the first I've heard of it."

Jean was skinning the peach and was smiling as at an amusing thought.

"I've been two years making up my mind to write it," she said, "and I'm going to dedicate it to Jack. I started work on it three or four days ago. Look at my wrist!" She held out her beautiful hand for the girl's inspection.

"It is a very pretty wrist," laughed Lydia, "but why did you want me to see it?"

"If you had a professional eye," said the girl, resuming her occupation, "you would have noticed the swelling, the result of writer's cramp."

"The yarn about your elderly admirer ought to provide a good chapter," said Jack, "and isn't there a phrase 'A Chapter of Accidents' – *that* ought to go in?"

She did not raise her eyes.

"Don't discourage me," she said a little sadly. "I have to make money somehow."

How much had she heard? Jack was wondering all the time, and he groaned inwardly when he saw how little effect his warning had upon the girl he was striving to protect. Women are natural actresses, but Lydia was not acting now. She was genuinely fond of Jean and he could see that she had accepted his warnings as the ravings of a diseased imagination. He confirmed this view when after a morning of sightseeing and the exploration of the spot where, two thousand years before, the Emperor Augustine had erected his lofty "trophy", they returned to the villa. There are some omissions which are marked, and when Lydia allowed him to depart without pressing him to stay to dinner he realised that he had lost the trick.

"When are you going back to London?" she asked.

"Tomorrow morning," said Jack. "I don't think I shall come here again before I go."

She did not reply immediately. She was a little penitent at her lack of hospitality, but Jack had annoyed her and the more convincing he had become, the greater had been the irritation he had caused. One question he had to ask but he hesitated.

"About that will – " he began, but her look of weariness stopped him.

It was a very annoyed young man that drove back to the Hôtel de Paris. He had hardly gone before Lydia regretted her brusqueness. She liked Jack Glover more than she was prepared to admit, and though he had only been in Cap Martin for two days she felt a little sense of desolation at his going. Very resolutely she refused even to consider his extraordinary views about Jean. And yet –

Jean left her alone and watched her strolling aimlessly about the garden, guessing the little storm which had developed in her breast. Lydia went to bed early that night, another significant sign Jean noted, and was not sorry, because she wanted to have her father to herself.

Mr Briggerland listened moodily whilst Jean related all that she had learnt, for she had been in the *salon* at the National for a good quarter of an hour before Jack had discovered her.

"I thought he would want her to make a will," she said, "and, of course, although she has rejected the idea now, it will grow on her. I think we have the best part of a week."

"I suppose you have everything cut and dried as usual," growled Mr Briggerland. "What is your plan?"

"I have three," said Jean thoughtfully, "and two are particularly appealing to me because they do not involve the employment of any third person."

"Had you one which brought in somebody else?" asked Briggerland in surprise. "I thought a clever girl like you – "

"Don't waste your sarcasm on me," said Jean quietly. "The third person whom I considered was Marcus Stepney," and she told him the gist of her conversation with the gambler. Mr Briggerland was not impressed.

"A thief like Marcus will get out of paying," he said, "and if he can stall you long enough to get the money you may whistle for your share. Besides, a fellow like that isn't really afraid of a charge of bigamy."

Jean, curled up in a big armchair, looked up under her eyelashes at her father and laughed.

"I had no intention of letting Marcus marry Lydia," she said coolly, "but I had to dangle something in front of his eyes, because he may serve me in quite another way."

"How did he get those two slashes on his hand?" asked Mr Briggerland suddenly.

"Ask him," she said. "Marcus is getting a little troublesome. I thought he had learnt his lesson and had realised that I am not built for matrimony, especially for a hectic attachment to a man who gains his livelihood by cheating at cards."

"Now, now, my dear," said her father.

"Please don't be shocked," she mocked him. "You know as well as I do how Marcus lives."

"The boy is very fond of you."

"The boy is between thirty and thirty-six," she said tersely. "And he's not the kind of boy that I am particularly fond of. He is useful and may be more useful yet."

She rose, stretched her arms and yawned.

"I'm going up to my room to work on my story. You are watching for Mr Jaggs?"

"Work on what?" he said.

"The story I am writing and which I think will create a sensation," she said calmly.

"What's this?" asked Briggerland suspiciously. "A story? I didn't know you were writing that kind of stuff."

"There are lots of important things that you know nothing about, parent," she said and left him a little dazed.

For once Jean was not deceiving him. A writing table had been put in her room and a thick pad of paper awaited her attention. She got into her kimono and with a little sigh sat down at the table and began to write. It was half past two when she gathered up the sheets and read them over with a smile which was half contempt. She was on the point of getting into bed when she remembered that her father was keeping watch below. She put on her slippers and went downstairs and tapped gently at the door of the darkened dining-room.

Almost immediately it was opened.

"What did you want to tap for?" he grumbled. "You gave me a start."

"I preferred tapping to being shot," she answered. "Have you heard anything or seen anybody?"

The French windows of the dining-room were open, her father was wearing his coat and on his arm she saw by the reflected starlight from outside he carried a shot gun.

"Nothing," he said. "The old man hasn't come tonight."

She nodded.

"Somehow I didn't think he would," she said.

"I don't see how I can shoot him without making a fuss."

"Don't be silly," said Jean lightly. "Aren't the police well aware that an elderly gentleman has threatened my life, and would it be remarkable if seeing an ancient man prowl about this house you shot him on sight?"

She bit her lips thoughtfully.

"Yes, I think you can go to bed," she said. "He will not be here tonight. Tomorrow night, yes."

She went up to her room, said her prayers and went to bed and was asleep immediately.

Lydia had forgotten about Jean's story until she saw her writing industriously at a small table which had been placed on the lawn. It was February, but the wind and the sun were warm and Lydia thought she had never seen a more beautiful picture than the girl presented sitting there in a garden spangled with gay flowers, heavy with the scent of February roses, a dainty figure of a girl, almost ethereal in her loveliness.

"Am I interrupting you?"

"Not a bit," said Jean, putting down her pen and rubbing her wrist. "Isn't it annoying. I've got to quite an exciting part, and my wrist is giving me hell."

She used the word so naturally that Lydia forgot to be shocked.

"Can I do anything for you?"

Jean shook her head.

"I don't exactly see what you can do," she said, "unless you could – but, no, I would not ask you to do that!"

"What is it?" asked Lydia.

Jean puckered her brows in thought.

"I suppose you could do it," she said, "but I'd hate to ask you. You see, dear, I've got a chapter to finish and it really ought to go off to London today. I am very keen on getting an opinion from a literary friend of mine – but, no, I won't ask you."

"What is it?" smiled Lydia. "I'm sure you're not going to ask the impossible."

"The thought occurred to me that perhaps you might write as I dictated. It would only be two or three pages," said the girl apologetically. "I'm so full of the story at this moment that it would be a shame if I allowed the divine fire of inspiration – that's the term, isn't it – to go out."

"Of course I'll do it," said Lydia. "I can't write shorthand, but that doesn't matter, does it?"

"No, longhand will be quick enough for me. My thoughts aren't so fast," said the girl.

"What is it all about?"

"It is about a girl," said Jean, "who has stolen a lot of money – "

"How thrilling!" smiled Lydia.

"And she's got away to America. She is living a very full and joyous life, but the thought of her sin is haunting her and she decides to disappear and let people think she has drowned herself. She is really going into a convent. I've got to the point where she is saying farewell to her friend. Do you feel capable of being harrowed?"

"I never felt fitter for the job in my life," said Lydia, and sitting down in the chair the girl had vacated, she took up the pencil which the other had left.

Jean strolled up and down the lawn in an agony of mental composition and presently she came back and began slowly to dictate.

Word by word Lydia wrote down the thrilling story of the girl's remorse, and presently came to the moment when the heroine was inditing a letter to her friend.

"Take a fresh page," said Jean, as Lydia paused halfway down one sheet. "I shall want to write something in there myself when my hand gets better. Now begin:

"MY DEAR FRIEND."

Lydia wrote down the words and slowly the girl dictated.

"I do not know how I can write you this letter. I intended to tell you when I saw you the other day how miserable I was. Your suspicion hurt me less than your ignorance of the one vital event in my life which has now made living a burden. My money has brought no joy to me. I have met a man I love, but with whom I know a union is impossible. We are determined to die together – farewell – "

"You said she was going away," interrupted Lydia.
"I know," Jean nodded. "Only she wants to give the impression – "
"I see, I see," said Lydia. "Go on."

"Forgive me for the act I am committing, which you may think is the act of a coward, and try to think as well of me as you possibly can. Your friend – "

"I don't know whether to make her sign her name or put her initials," said Jean, pursing her lips.
"What is her name?"
"Laura Martin. Just put the initials L M."
"They're mine also," smiled Lydia. "What else?"
"I don't think I'll do any more," said Jean. "I'm not a good dictator, am I? Though you're a wonderful amanuensis."
She collected the papers tidily, put them in a little portfolio and tucked them under her arm.
"Let us gamble the afternoon away," said Jean. "I want distraction."
"But your story? Haven't you to send it off?"
"I'm going to wrestle with it in secret, even if it breaks my wrist," said Jean brightly.
She took the portfolio up to her room, locked the door and sorted over the pages. The page which held the farewell letter she put

carefully aside. The remainder, including all that part of the story she had written on the previous night, she made into a bundle, and when Lydia had gone off with Marcus Stepney to swim, she carried the paper to a remote corner of the grounds and burnt it sheet by sheet. Again she examined the "letter," folded it and locked it in a drawer.

Lydia, returning from her swim, was met by Jean halfway up the hill.

"By the way, my dear, I wish you would give me Jack Glover's London address," she said as they went into the house. "Write it here. Here is a pencil." She pulled out an envelope from a stationery rack and Lydia, in all innocence, wrote as she requested.

The envelope Jean carried upstairs, put into it the letter signed "L M," and sealed it down. Lydia Meredith was nearer to death at that moment than she had been on the afternoon when Mordon the chauffeur brought his big Fiat on to the pavement of Berkeley Street.

29

It was in the evening of the next day that Lydia received a wire from Jack Glover. It was addressed from London and announced his arrival.

"Doesn't it make you feel nice, Lydia," said Jean, when she saw the telegram, "to have a man in London looking after your interests – a sort of guardian angel – and another guardian angel prowling round your demesne at Cap Martin?"

"You mean Jaggs? Have you seen him?"

"No, I have not seen him," said the girl softly. "I should rather like to see him. Do you know where he is staying at Monte Carlo?"

Lydia shook her head.

"I hope I shall see him before I go," said Jean. "He must be a very interesting old gentleman."

It was Mr Briggerland who first caught a glimpse of Lydia's watchman. Mr Briggerland had spent the greater part of the day sleeping. He was unusually wakeful at one o'clock in the morning, and sat on the veranda in a fur-lined overcoat, his gun lay across his knees. He had seen many mysterious shapes flitting across the lawn, only to discover on investigation that they were no more than the shadows which the moving treetops cast.

At two o'clock he saw a shape emerge from the tree belt and move stealthily in the shadow of the bushes toward the house. He did not fire because there was a chance that it might have been one of the detectives who had promised to keep an eye upon the Villa Casa in view of the murderous threats which Jean had received.

Noiselessly he rose and stepped in his rubber shoes to the darker end of the stoep. It was old Jaggs. There was no mistaking him. A bent man who limped cautiously across the lawn and was making for the back of the house. Mr Briggerland cocked his gun and took aim…

Both girls heard the shot, and Lydia, springing out of bed, ran on to the balcony.

"It's all right, Mrs Meredith," said Briggerland's voice. "It was a burglar, I think."

"You haven't hurt him?" she cried, remembering old Jaggs' nocturnal habits.

"If I have, he's got away," said Briggerland. "He must have seen me and dropped."

Jean flew downstairs in her dressing gown and joined her father on the lawn.

"Did you get him?" she asked in a low voice.

"I could have sworn I shot him," said her father in the same tone, "but the old devil must have dropped."

He heard the quick catch of her breath and turned apprehensively.

"Now, don't make a fuss about it, Jean, I couldn't help it."

"You couldn't help it!" she almost snarled. "You had him under your gun and you let him go. Do you think he'll ever come again, you fool?"

"Now look here, I'm not going to – " began Mr Briggerland, but she snatched the gun from his hand, looked swiftly at the lock and ran across the lawn toward the trees.

Somebody was hiding. She sensed that and all her nerves were alert. Presently she saw a crouching figure and lifted the gun, but before she could fire it was wrested from her hand.

She opened her lips to cry out for help, but a hand closed over her mouth, and swung her round so that her back was toward her assailant, and then in a flash his arm came round her neck, the flex of the elbow against her throat.

"Say one of them prayers of yours," said a voice in her ear, and the arm tightened.

She struggled furiously, but the man held her as though she were a child.

"You're going to die," whispered the voice. "How do you like the sensation?"

The arm tightened on her neck. She was suffocating, dying she thought, and her heart was filled with a wild, mad longing for life and a terror undreamt of. She could faintly hear her father's voice calling her and then consciousness departed.

When Jean came to herself she was in Lydia Meredith's arms. She opened her eyes and saw the pathetic face of her father looming from the background. Her hand went up to her throat.

"Hallo, people – how did I get here?" she asked as she struggled into a sitting position.

"I came in search of you and found you lying on the ground," quavered Mr Briggerland.

"Did you see the man?" she asked.

"No. What happened to you, darling?"

"Nothing," she said with that composure which she could command. "I must have fainted. It was rather ridiculous of me, wasn't it?" she smiled.

She got unsteadily to her feet and again she felt her throat. Lydia noticed the action.

"Did he hurt you?" she asked anxiously. "It couldn't have been Jaggs."

"Oh no," smiled Jean, "it couldn't have been Jaggs. I think I'll go to bed."

She did not expect to sleep. For the first time in her extraordinary life fear had come to her, and she had shivered on the very edge of the abyss. She felt the shudder she could not repress and shook herself impatiently. Then she extinguished the light and went to the window and looked out. Somewhere there in the darkness she knew her enemy was hidden, and again that sense of apprehension swept over her.

"I'm losing my nerve," she murmured.

143

It was extraordinary to Lydia Meredith that the girl showed no sign of her night's adventure when she came in to breakfast on the following morning. She looked bright. Her eyes were clear and her delicate irony as pointed as though she had slept the clock round.

Lydia did not swim that day, and Mr Stepney had his journey out to Cap Martin in vain. Nor was she inclined to go back with him to Monte Carlo to the Casino in the afternoon, and Mr Stepney began to realise that he was wasting valuable time.

Jean found her scribbling in the garden and Lydia made no secret of the task she was undertaking.

"Making your will? What a grisly idea?" she said as she put down the cup of tea she had carried out to the girl.

"Isn't it," said Lydia with a grimace. "It is the most worrying business, too, Jean. There is nobody I want to leave money to except you and Mr Glover."

"For heaven's sake don't leave me any or Jack will think I am conspiring to bring about your untimely end," said Jean. "Why make a will at all?"

There was no need for her to ask that, but she was curious to discover what reply the girl would make, and to her surprise Lydia fenced with the question.

"It is done in all the best circles," she said good-humouredly. "And, Jean, I'm not interested in a single public institution! I don't know by title the name of any home for dogs, and I shouldn't be at all anxious to leave my money to one even if I did."

"Then you'd better leave it to Jack Glover," said the girl, "or to the Lifeboat Institution."

Lydia threw down her pencil in disgust.

"Fancy making one's will on a beautiful day like this, and giving instructions as to where one should be buried. Brrr! Jean," she asked suddenly, "was it Mr Jaggs you saw in the wood?"

Jean shook her head.

"I saw nobody," she said. "I went in to look for the burglar; the excitement must have been too much for me, and I fainted."

But Lydia was not satisfied.

"I can't understand Mr Jaggs myself," she said, but Jean interrupted her with a cry.

Lydia looked up and saw her eyes shining and her lips parting in a smile.

"Of course," she said softly. "He used to sleep at your flat, didn't he?"

"Yes, why?" asked the girl in surprise.

"What a fool I am, what a perfect fool!" said Jean, startled out of her accustomed self-possession.

"I don't quite know where your folly comes in, but perhaps you will tell me," but Jean was laughing softly.

"Go on and make your will," she said mockingly. "And when you've finished we'll go into the rooms and chase the lucky numbers. Poor dear Mrs Cole-Mortimer is feeling a little neglected, too, we ought to do something for her."

The day and night passed without any untoward event. In the evening Jean had an interview with her French chauffeur, and afterwards disappeared into her room. Lydia tapping at her door to bid her goodnight received no answer.

Day was breaking when old Jaggs came out from the trees in his furtive way and glancing up and down the road made his halting way toward Monte Carlo. The only objects in sight was a donkey laden with market produce led by a bare-legged boy who was going in the same direction as he.

A little more than a mile along the road he turned sharply to the right and began climbing a steep and narrow bridle path which joined the mountain road, halfway up to La Turbie. The boy with the donkey turned off to the main road and continued the steep climb toward the Grande Corniche. There were many houses built on the edge of the road and practically on the edge of precipices, for the windows facing the sea often looked sheer down for two hundred feet. At first these dwellings appeared in clusters, then as the road climbed higher, they occurred at rare intervals.

The boy leading the donkey kept his eye upon the valley below, and from time to time caught a glimpse of the old man who had now left the bridle path, and was picking his way up the rough hill-side. He was making for a dilapidated house which stood at one of the hairpin bends of the road, and the donkey-boy, shading his eyes from the glare of the rising sun, saw him disappear into what must have been the cellar of the house, since the door through which he went was a good twenty feet beneath the level of the road. The donkey-boy continued his climb, tugging at his burdened beast, and presently he came up to the house. Smoke was rising from one of the chimneys, and he halted at the door, tied the rope he held to a rickety gatepost, and knocked gently.

A bright-faced peasant woman came to the open door and shook her head at the sight of the wares with which the donkey was laden.

"We want none of your truck, my boy," she said. "I have my own garden. You are not a Monogasque."

"No, signora," replied the boy, flashing his teeth with a smile. "I am from San Remo, but I have come to live in Monte Carlo to sell vegetables for my uncle, and he told me I should find a lodging here."

She looked at him dubiously.

"I have one room which you could have, boy," she said, "though I do not like Italians. You must pay me a franc a night, and your donkey can go into the shed of my brother-in-law up the hill."

She led the way down a flight of ancient stairs and showed him a tiny room overlooking the valley.

"I have one other man who lives here," she said. "An old one, who sleeps all day and goes out all night. But he is a very respectable man," she added in defence of her client.

"Where does he sleep?" asked the boy.

"There!" The woman pointed to a room on the opposite side of the narrow landing. "He has just come in, I can hear him." She listened.

"Will madame get me change for this?" The boy produced a fifty-franc note, and the woman's eyebrows rose.

"Such wealth!" she said good-naturedly. "I did not think that a little boy like you could have such money."

146

She bustled upstairs to her own room, leaving the boy alone. He waited until her heavy footsteps sounded overhead, and then gently he tried the door of the other lodger. Mr Jaggs had not yet bolted the door, and the spy pushed it open and looked. What he saw satisfied him, for he pulled the door tight again, and as the footfall of old Jaggs came nearer the door, the donkey-boy flew upstairs with extraordinary rapidity.

"I will come later, madame," he said, when he had received the change. "I must take my donkey into Monte Carlo."

She watched the boy and his beast go down the road, and went back to the task of preparing her lodger's breakfast.

To Monte Carlo the cabbage seller did not go. Instead, he turned back the way he had come, and a hundred yards from the gate of Villa Casa, Mordon, the chauffeur, appeared, and took the rope from his hand.

"Did you find what you wanted, mademoiselle?" he asked.

Jean nodded. She got into the house through the servants' entrance and up to her room without observation. She pulled off the black wig and applied herself to removing the stains from her face. It had been a good morning's work.

"You must keep Mrs Meredith fully occupied today." She waylaid her father on the stairs to give him these instructions.

For her it was a busy morning. First she went to the Hôtel de Paris, and on the pretext of writing a letter in the lounge secured two or three sheets of the hotel paper and an envelope. Next she hired a typewriter and carried it with her back to the house. She was working for an hour before she had the letter finished. The signature took her some time. She had to ransack Lydia's writing case before she found a letter from Jack Glover – Lydia's signature was easy in comparison.

This, and a cheque drawn from the back of Lydia Meredith's chequebook, completed her equipment.

That afternoon Mordon, the chauffeur, motored into Nice, and by nine o'clock that night an aeroplane deposited him in Paris. He was in London the following morning, a bearer of an urgent letter to Mr Rennett, the lawyer, which, however, he did not present in person.

147

Mordon knew a French girl in London, and she it was who carried the letter to Charles Rennett – a letter that made him scratch his head many times before he took a sheet of paper, and addressing the manager of Lydia's bank, wrote: "This cheque is in order. Please honour."

30

"Desperate diseases," said Jean Briggerland, "call for desperate remedies."

Mr Briggerland looked up from his book. "What was that tale you were telling Lydia this morning," he asked, "about Glover's gambling? He was only here a day, wasn't he?"

"He was here long enough to lose a lot of money," said Jean. "Of course he didn't gamble, so he did not lose. It was just a little seed-sowing on my part – one never knows how useful the right word may be in the right season."

"Did you tell Lydia that he was losing heavily?" he asked quickly.

"Am I a fool? Of course not! I merely said that youth would be served, and if you have the gambling instinct in you, why, it didn't matter what position you held in society or what your responsibilities were, you must indulge your passion."

Mr Briggerland stroked his chin. There were times when Jean's schemes got very far beyond him, and he hated the mental exercise of catching up. The only thing he knew was that every post from London bore urgent demands for money, and that the future held possibilities which he did not care to contemplate. He was in the unfortunate position of having numerous pensioners to support, men and women who had served him in various ways and whose approval, but what was more important, whose loyalty, depended largely upon the regularity of their payments.

"I shall gamble or do something desperate," he said with a frown. "Unless you can bring off a coup that will produce twenty thousand pounds of ready money we are going to get into all kinds of trouble, Jean."

"Do you think I don't know that?" she asked contemptuously. "It is because of this urgent need of money that I have taken a step which I hate."

He listened in amazement whilst she told him what she had done to relieve her pressing needs.

"We are getting deeper and deeper into Mordon's hands," he said, shaking his head. "That is what scares me at times."

"You needn't worry about Mordon," she smiled. Her smile was a little hard. "Mordon and I are going to be married."

She was examining the toe of her shoe attentively as she spoke, and Mr Briggerland leapt to his feet.

"What!" he squeaked. "Marry a chauffeur? A fellow I picked out of the gutter? You're mad! The fellow is a rascal who has earned the guillotine time and time again."

"Who hasn't?" she asked, looking up.

"It is incredible! It's madness!" he said.

"I had no idea – " he stopped for want of breath.

Mordon was becoming troublesome. She had known that better than her father.

"It was after the 'accident' that didn't happen that he began to get a little tiresome," she said. "You say we are getting deeper and deeper into his hands? Well, he hinted as much, and I did not like it. When he began to get a little loving I accepted that way out as an easy alternative to a very unpleasant exposure. Whether he would have betrayed us I don't know; probably he would."

Mr Briggerland's face was dark.

"When is this interesting event to take place?"

"My marriage? In two months, I think. When is Easter? That class of person always wants to be married at Easter. I asked him to keep our secret and not to mention it to you, and I should not have spoken now if you had not referred to the obligation we were under."

"In two months?" Mr Briggerland nodded. "Let me know when you want this to end, Jean," he said.

"It will end almost immediately. Please do not trouble," said Jean, "and there is one other thing, father. If you see Mr Jaggs in the garden tonight, I beg of you do not attempt to shoot him. He is a very useful man."

Her father sank back in his chair.

"You're beyond me," he said, helplessly. Mordon occupied two rooms above the garage, which was conveniently situated for Jean's purpose. He arrived late the next night, and a light in his window, which was visible from the girl's room, told her all she wanted to know.

Mr Mordon was a good-looking man by certain standards. His hair was dark and glossily brushed. His normal pallor of countenance gave him the interesting appearance which men of his kind did not greatly dislike, and he had a figure which was admired in a dozen servants' halls, and a manner which passed amongst housemaids for "gentlemanly", and amongst gentlemen as "superior". He heard the foot of the girl on the stairs, and opened the door.

"You have brought it?" she said, without a preliminary word.

She had thrown a dark cloak over her evening dress, and the man's eyes feasted on her.

"Yes, I have brought it – Jean," he said.

She put her finger to her lips.

"Be careful, François," she cautioned in a low voice.

Although the man spoke English as well as he spoke French, it was in the latter language that the conversation was carried on. He went to a grip which lay on the bed, opened it and took out five thick packages of thousand-franc notes.

"There are a thousand in each, mademoiselle. Five million francs. I changed part of the money in Paris, and part in London."

"The woman – there is no danger from her?"

"Oh no, mademoiselle," he smiled complacently. "She is not likely to betray me, and she does not know my name or where I am living. She is a girl I met at a dance at the Swiss Waiters' Club," he explained. "She is not a good character. I think the French police wish to find her, but she is very clever."

"What did you tell her?" asked Jean.

"That I was working a coup with Vaud and Montheron. These are two notorious men in Paris whom she knew. I gave her five thousand francs for her work."

"There was no trouble?"

"None whatever, mademoiselle. I watched her, and saw she carried the letter to the bank. As soon as the money was changed I left Croydon by air for Paris, and came on from Paris to Marseilles by aeroplane."

"You did well, François," she said, and patted his hand.

He would have seized hers, but she drew back.

"You have promised, François," she said with dignity, "and a French gentleman keeps his word."

François bowed.

He was not a French gentleman, but he was anxious that this girl should think he was, and to that end had told her stories of his birth which had apparently impressed her.

"Now will you do something more for me?"

"I will do anything in the world, Jean," he cried passionately, and again a restraining hand fell on his shoulder.

"Then sit down and write; your French is so much better than mine."

"What shall I write?" he asked. She had never called upon him for proof of his scholarship, and he was childishly eager to reveal to the woman he loved attainments of which he had no knowledge.

"Write, 'Dear Mademoiselle'." He obeyed.

" 'I have returned from London, and have confessed to Madame Meredith that I have forged her name and have drawn £100,000 from her bank –' "

"Why do I write this, Jean?" he asked in surprise.

"I will tell you one day – go on, François," she continued her dictation.

" 'And now I have learnt that Madame Meredith loves me. There is only one end to this – that which you see – ' "

"Do you intend passing suspicion to somebody else?" he asked, evidently fogged, "but why should I say – ?"

She stopped his mouth with her hand.

"How wonderful you are, Jean," he said, admiringly, as he blotted the paper and handed it to her. "So that if this matter is traced to you – " She looked into his eyes and smiled.

"There will be trouble for somebody," she said, softly, as she put the paper in her pocket.

Suddenly, before she could realise what was happening he had her in his arms, his lips pressed against hers.

"Jean, Jean!" he muttered. "You adorable woman!"

Gently she pressed him back and she was still smiling, though her eyes were like granite.

"Gently, François," she said, "you must have patience!"

She slipped through the door and closed it behind her, and even in her then state of mind she did not slam it, nor did she hurry down the stairs, but went out, taking her time, and was back in the house without her absence having been noticed. Her face, reflected in her long mirror, was serene in its repose, but within her a devil was alive, hungry for destruction. No man had roused the love of Jean Briggerland, but at least one had succeeded in bringing to life a consuming hate which, for the time being, absorbed her.

From the moment she drew her wet handkerchief across her red lips and flung the dainty thing as though it were contaminated through the open window, François Mordon was a dead man.

31

A letter from Jack Glover arrived the next morning. He had had an easy journey, was glad to have had the opportunity of seeing Lydia, and hoped she would think over the will. Lydia was not thinking of wills, but of an excuse to get back to London. Of a sudden the loveliness of Monte Carlo had palled upon her, and she had almost forgotten the circumstances which had made the change of scene and climate so welcome.

"Go back to London, my dear?" said Mrs Cole-Mortimer, shocked. "What a – a rash notion! Why it is freezing in town and foggy and...and I really can't let you go back!"

Mrs Cole-Mortimer was agitated at the very thought. Her own good time on the Riviera depended upon Lydia staying. Jean had made that point very clear. She, herself, she explained to her discomforted hostess, was ready to go back at once, and the prolongation of Mrs Cole-Mortimer's stay depended upon Lydia's plans. A startling switch of cause and effect, for Mrs Cole-Mortimer had understood that Jean's will controlled the plans of the party.

Lydia might have insisted, had she really known the reason for her sudden longing for the grimy metropolis. But she could not even convince herself that the charms of Monte Carlo were contingent upon the presence there of a man who had aroused her furious indignation and with whom she had spent most of the time quarrelling. She mentioned her unrest to Jean, and Jean as usual seemed to understand.

"The Riviera is rather like Turkish Delight – very sweet, but unsatisfying," she said. "Stay another week and then if you feel that way we'll all go home together."

"This means breaking up your holiday," said Lydia in self-reproach.

"Not a bit," denied the girl, "perhaps I shall feel as you do in a week's time."

A week! Jean thought that much might happen in a week. In truth events began to move quickly from that night, but in a way she had not anticipated.

Mr Briggerland, who had been reading the newspaper through the conversation, looked up.

"They are making a great fuss of this Moor in Nice," he said, "but if I remember rightly, Nice invariably has some weird lion to adore."

"Muley Hafiz," said Lydia. "Yes, I saw him the day I went to lunch with Mr Stepney, a fine-looking man."

"I'm not greatly interested in natives," said Jean carelessly. "What is he, a Negro?"

"Oh, no, he's fairer than – " Lydia was about to say "your father", but thought it discreet to find another comparison. "He's fairer than most of the people in the south of France," she said, "but then all very highly bred Moors are, aren't they?"

Jean shook her head.

"Ethnology means nothing to me," she said humorously. "I've got my idea of Moors from Shakespeare, and I thought they were mostly black. What is he then? I haven't read the papers."

"He is the Pretender to the Moorish throne," said Lydia, "and there has been a lot of trouble in the French Senate about him. France supports his claims, and the Spaniards have offered a reward for his body, dead or alive, and that has brought about a strained relationship between Spain and France."

Jean regarded her with an amused smile.

"Fancy taking an interest in international politics. I suppose that is due to your working on a newspaper, Lydia."

Jean discovered that she was to take a greater interest in Muley Hafiz than she could have thought was possible. She had to go into

Monte Carlo to do some shopping. Menton was nearer, but she preferred the drive into the principality.

The Rooms had no great call for her, and whilst Mordon went to a garage to have a faulty cylinder examined, she strolled on to the terrace of the Casino, down the broad steps towards the sea. The bathing huts were closed at this season, but the little road down to the beach is secluded and had been a favourite walk of hers in earlier visits.

Near the huts she passed a group of dark-looking men in long white jellabs, and wondered which of these was the famous Muley. One she noticed with a particularly negro type of face wore on his flowing robe the scarlet ribbon of the Legion of Honour. Somehow or other he did not seem interesting enough to be Muley, she thought, as she went on to a strip of beach.

A man was standing on the seashore, a tall, commanding man, gazing out it seemed across the sunlit ocean as though he were in search of something. He could not have heard her footfall because she was walking on the sand, and yet he must have realised her presence, for he turned, and she almost stopped at the sight of his face. He might have been a European; his complexion was fair, though his eyebrows and eyes were jet black, as also was the tiny beard and moustache he wore. Beneath the conventional jellab he wore a dark green jacket, and she had a glimpse of glittering decorations before he pulled over his cloak so that they were hidden. But it was his eyes which held her. They were large and as black as night, and they were set in a face of such strength and dignity that Jean knew instinctively that she was looking upon the Moorish Pretender.

They stood for a second staring at one another, and then the Moor stepped aside.

"Pardon," he said in French, "I am afraid I startled you."

Jean was breathing a little quicker. She could not remember in her life any man who had created so immediate and favourable an impression. She forgot her contempt for native people, forgot his race, his religion (and religion was a big thing to Jean), forgot everything except that behind those eyes she recognised something which was kin to her.

"You are English, of course," he said in that language.

"Scottish," smiled Jean.

"It is almost the same, isn't it?" He spoke without any trace of an accent, without an error of grammar, and his voice was the voice of a college man.

He had left the way open for her to pass on, but she lingered.

"You are Muley Hafiz, aren't you?" she asked, and he turned his head. "I've read a great deal about you," she added, though in truth she had read nothing.

He laughed, showing two rows of perfect white teeth. It was only by contrast with their whiteness that she noticed the golden brown of his complexion.

"I am of international interest," he said lightly and glanced round toward his attendants.

She thought he was going and would have moved on, but he stopped her.

"You are the first English speaking person I have talked to since I've been in France," he said, "except the American Ambassador." He smiled as at a pleasant recollection.

"You talk almost like an Englishman yourself."

"I was at Oxford," he said. "My brother was at Harvard. My father, the brother of the late Sultan, was a very progressive man and believed in the Western education for his children. Won't you sit down?" he asked, pointing to the sand.

She hesitated a second, and then sank to the ground, and crossing his legs he sat by her side.

"I was in France for four years," he carried on, evidently anxious to hold her in conversation, "so I speak both languages fairly well. Do you speak Arabic?" He asked the question solemnly, but his eyes were bright with laughter.

"Not very well," she answered gravely.

"Are you staying very long?" It was a conventional question and she was unprepared for the reply.

"I leave tonight," he said, "though very few people know it. You have surprised a State secret," he smiled again.

And then he began to talk of Morocco and its history, and with extraordinary ease he traced the story of the families which had ruled that troubled State.

He touched lightly on his own share in the rebellion which had almost brought about a European war.

"My uncle seized the throne, you know," he said, taking up a handful of sand and tossing it up in the air. "He defeated my father and killed him, and then we caught his two sons."

"What happened to them?" asked Jean curiously.

"Oh, we killed them," he said carelessly. "I had them hanged in front of my tent. You're shocked?"

She shook her head.

"Do you believe in killing your enemies?"

She nodded.

"Why not? It is the only logical thing to do."

"My brother joined forces with the present Sultan, and if I ever catch him I shall hang him too," he smiled.

"And if he catches you?" she asked.

"Why, he'll hang me," he laughed. "That is the rule of the game."

"How strange!" she said, half to herself.

"Do you think so? I suppose from the European standpoint – "

"No, no," she stopped him. "I wasn't thinking of that. You are logical and you do the logical thing. That is how I would treat my enemies."

"If you had any," he suggested.

She nodded.

"If I had any," she repeated with a hard little smile. "Will you tell me this – do I call you Mr Muley or Lord Muley?"

"You may call me Wazeer, if you're so hard up for a title," he said, and the little idiom sounded queer from him.

"Well, Wazeer, will you tell me: Suppose somebody who had something that you wanted very badly and they wouldn't give it to you, and you had the power to destroy them, what would you do?"

"I should certainly destroy them," said Muley Hafiz. "It is unnecessary to ask. 'The common rule, the simple plan'," he quoted.

Her eyes were fixed on his face, and she was frowning, though this she did not know.

"I am glad I met you this afternoon," she said. "It must be wonderful living in that atmosphere, the atmosphere of might and power, where men and women aren't governed by the finicking rules which vitiate the Western world."

He laughed.

"Then you are tired of your Western civilisation," he said as he rose and helped her to her feet (his hands were long and delicate, and she grew breathless at the touch of them). "You must come along to my little city in the hills where the law is the sword of Muley Hafiz."

She looked at him for a moment.

"I almost wish I could," she said and held out her hand.

He took it in the European fashion and bowed over it. She seemed so tiny a thing by the side of him, her head did not reach his shoulder.

"Goodbye," she said hurriedly and turning, walked back the way she had come, and he stood watching her until she was out of sight.

32

"Jean!"

She looked round to meet the scowling gaze of Marcus Stepney.

"I must say you're the limit," he said violently. "There are lots of things I imagine you'd do, but to stand there in broad daylight talking to a nigger – "

"If I stand in broad daylight and talk to a card-sharper, Marcus, I think I'm just low enough to do almost anything."

"A damned Moorish nigger," he spluttered, and her eyes narrowed.

"Walk up the road with me, and if you possibly can, keep your voice down to the level which gentlemen usually employ when talking to women," she said.

She was in better condition than he, and he was a little out of breath by the time they reached the Café de Paris, which was crowded at that hour with the afternoon tea people.

He found a quiet corner, and by this time his anger, and a little of his courage, had evaporated.

"I've only your interest at heart, Jean," he said almost pleadingly, "but you don't want people in our set to know you've been hobnobbing with this infernal Moor."

"When you say 'our set', to which set are you referring?" she asked unpleasantly. "Because if it is the set I believe you mean, they can't think too badly of me for my liking. It would be a degradation to me to be admired by your set, Marcus."

"Oh, come now," he began feebly.

"I thought I had made it clear to you and I hoped you would carry the marks to your dying day" – there was malice in her voice, and he winced – "that I do not allow you to dominate my life or to censor my actions. The 'nigger' you referred to was more of a gentleman than you can ever be, Marcus, because he has breed, which the Lord didn't give to you."

The waiter brought the tea at that moment, and the conversation passed to unimportant topics till he had gone.

"I'm rather rattled," he apologised. "I lost six thousand louis last night."

"Then you have six thousand reasons why you should keep on good terms with me," said Jean smiling cheerfully.

"That caveman stuff?" he asked, and shook his head. "She'd raise Cain."

Jean was laughing inside herself, but she did not show her merriment.

"You can but try," she said. "I've already told you how it can be done."

"I'll try tomorrow," he said after a thought. "By heavens, I'll try to-morrow!"

It was on the tip of her tongue to say "Not tomorrow," but she checked herself.

Mordon came round with the car to pick her up soon after. Mordon! Her little chin jerked up with a gesture of annoyance, which she seldom permitted herself. And yet she felt unusually cheered. Her meeting with the Moor was a milestone in her life from which memory she could draw both encouragement and comfort.

"You met Muley?" said Lydia. "How thrilling! What is he like, Jean? Was he a blackamoor?"

"No, he wasn't a blackamoor," said the girl quietly. "He was an unusually intelligent man."

"H'm," grunted her father. "How did you come to meet him, my dear?"

"I picked him up on the beach," said Jean coolly, "as any flapper would pick up any nut."

Mr Briggerland choked.

"I hate to hear you talking like that, Jean. Who introduced him?"

"I told you," she said complacently. "I introduced myself. I talked to him on the beach and he talked to me, and we sat down and played with the sand and discussed one another's lives."

"But how enterprising of you, Jean," said the admiring Lydia.

Mr Briggerland was going to say something, but thought better of it.

There was a concert at the theatre that night and the whole party went. They had a box, and the interval had come before Lydia saw somebody ushered into a box on the other side of the house with such evidence of deference that she would have known who he was even if she had not seen the scarlet fez and the white robe.

"It is your Muley," she whispered.

Jean looked round.

Muley Hafiz was looking across at her; his eyes immediately sought the girl's, and he bowed slightly.

"What the devil is he bowing at?" grumbled Mr Briggerland. "You didn't take any notice of him, did you, Jean?"

"I bowed to him," said his daughter, not troubling to look round. "Don't be silly, father; anyway, if he weren't nice, it would be quite the right thing to do. I'm the most distinguished woman in the house because I know Muley Hafiz, and he has bowed to mě! Don't you realise the social value of a lion's recognition?"

Lydia could not see him distinctly. She had an impression of a white face, two large black spaces where his eyes were and a black beard. He sat all the time in the shadow of a curtain.

Jean looked round to see if Marcus Stepney was present, hoping that he had witnessed the exchange of courtesies, but Marcus at that moment was watching little bundles of twelve thousand franc notes raked across to the croupier's end of the table – which is the business end of Monte Carlo.

Jean was the last to leave the car when it set them down at the Villa Casa. Mordon called her respectfully.

"Excuse me, mademoiselle," he said, "I wish you would come to the garage and see the new tyres that have arrived. I don't like them."

It was a code which she had agreed he should use when he wanted her.

"Very good, Mordon, I will come to the garage later," she said carelessly.

"What does Mordon want you for?" asked her father, with a frown.

"You heard him. He doesn't approve of some new tyres that have been bought for the car," she said coolly. "And don't ask me questions. I've got a headache and I'm dying for a cup of chocolate."

"If that fellow gives you any trouble he'll be sorry," said Briggerland. "And let me tell you this, Jean, that marriage idea of yours – "

She only looked at him, but he knew the look and wilted.

"I don't want to interfere with your private affairs," he mumbled, "but the very thought of it gets me crazy."

The garage was a brick building erected by the side of the carriage drive, built much nearer the house than is usually the case.

Jean waited a reasonable time before she slipped away. Mordon was waiting for her before the open doors of the garage. The place was in darkness; she did not see him standing in the entrance until she was within a few paces of the man.

"Come up to my room," he said briskly.

"What do you want?" she asked.

"I want to speak to you and this is not the place."

"This is the only place where I am prepared to speak to you at the moment, François," she said reproachfully. "Don't you realise that my father is within hearing, and at any moment Madame Meredith may come out? How would I explain my presence in your room?"

He did not answer for the moment, then: "Jean, I am worried," he said, in a troubled voice. "I cannot understand your plans – they are too clever for me, and I have known men and women of great attainment. The great Bersac – "

163

"The great Bersac is dead," she said coldly. "He was a man of such great attainments that he came to the knife. Besides, it is not necessary that you should understand my plans, François."

She knew quite well what was troubling him, but she waited.

"I cannot understand the letter which I wrote for you," said Mordon. "The letter in which I say Madame Meredith loved me. I have thought this matter out, Jean, and it seems to me that I am compromised."

She laughed softly.

"Poor François," she said mockingly. "With whom could you be compromised but with your future wife? If I desire you to write that letter, what else matters?"

Again he was silent.

"I cannot speak here," he said almost roughly. "You must come to my room."

She hesitated. There was something in his voice she did not like.

"Very well," she said, and followed him up the steep stairs.

33

"Now explain." His words were a command, his tone peremptory.

Jean, who knew men, and read them without error, realised that this was not a moment to temporise.

"I will explain to you, François, but I do not like the way you speak," she said. "It is not you I wish to compromise, but Madame Meredith."

"In this letter I wrote for you I said I was going away. I confessed to you that I had forged a cheque for five million francs. That is a very serious document, mademoiselle, to be in the possession of anybody but myself." He looked at her straight in the eyes and she met his gaze unflinchingly.

"The thing will be made very clear to you tomorrow, François," she said softly, "and really there is no reason to worry. I wish to end this unhappy state of affairs."

"With me?" he asked quickly.

"No, with Madame Meredith," she answered. "I, too, am tired of waiting for marriage and I intend asking my father's permission for the wedding to take place next week. Indeed, François," she lowered her eyes modestly, "I have already written to the British Consul at Nice, asking him to arrange for the ceremony to be performed."

The sallow face of the chauffeur flushed a dull red.

"Do you mean that?" he said eagerly. "Jean, you are not deceiving me?"

She shook her head.

"No, François," she said in that low plaintive voice of hers, "I could not deceive you in a matter so important to myself."

He stood watching her, his breast heaving, his burning eyes devouring her, then: "You will give me back that letter I wrote, Jean?" he said.

"I will give it to you tomorrow."

"Tonight," he said, and took both her hands in his. "I am sure I am right. It is too dangerous a letter to be in existence, Jean, dangerous for you and for me – you will let me have it tonight?"

She hesitated.

"It is in my room," she said, an unnecessary statement, and, in the circumstances, a dangerous one, for his eyes dropped to the bag that hung at her wrist.

"It is there," he said. "Jean darling, do as I ask," he pleaded. "You know, every time I think of that letter I go cold. I was a madman when I wrote it."

"I have not got it here," she said steadily. She tried to draw back, but she was too late. He gripped her wrists and pulled the bag roughly from her hand.

"Forgive me, but I know I am right," he began, and then like a fury she flew at him, wrenched the bag from his hand, and by the very violence of her attack flung him backward.

He stared at her, and the colour faded from his face leaving it a dead white.

"What is this you are trying to do?" he glowered at her.

"I will see you in the morning, François," she said and turned.

Before she could reach the head of the stairs his arm was round her and he had dragged her back.

"My friend," he said between his teeth, "there is something in this matter which is bad for me."

"Let me go," she breathed and struck at his face.

For a full minute they struggled, and then the door opened and Mr Briggerland came in, and at the sight of his livid face, Mordon released his hold.

"You swine!" hissed the big man. His fist shot out and Mordon went down with a crash to the ground. For a moment he was stunned, and then with a snarl he turned over on his side and whipped a revolver from his hip pocket. Before he could fire, the girl had gripped the pistol and wrenched it from his hand.

"Get up," said Briggerland sternly. "Now explain to me, my friend, what you mean by this disgraceful attack upon mademoiselle."

The man rose and dusted himself mechanically and there was that in his face which boded no good to Mr Briggerland.

Before he could speak Jean intervened.

"Father," she said quietly, "you have no right to strike François."

"François," spluttered Briggerland, his dark face purple with rage.

"François," she repeated calmly. "It is right that you should know that François and I will be married next week."

Mr Briggerland's jaw dropped.

"What?" he almost shrieked.

She nodded.

"We are going to be married next week," she said, "and the little scene you witnessed has nothing whatever to do with you."

The effect of these words on Mordon was magical. The malignant frown which had distorted his face cleared away. He looked from Jean to Briggerland as though it were impossible to believe the evidence of his ears.

"François and I love one another," Jean went on in her even voice. "We have quarrelled tonight on a matter which has nothing to do with anybody save ourselves."

"You're – going – to – marry – him – next – week?" said Mr Briggerland dully. "By God, you'll do nothing of the sort!"

She raised her hand.

"It is too late for you to interfere, father," she said quietly. "François and I shall go our way and face our own fate. I'm sorry you disapprove, because you have always been a very loving father to me."

That was the first hint Mr Briggerland had received that there might be some other explanation for her words, and he became calmer.

"Very well," he said, "I can only tell you that I strongly disapprove of the action you have taken and that I shall do nothing whatever to further your reckless scheme. But I must insist upon your coming back to the house now. I cannot have my daughter talked about."

She nodded.

"I will see you tomorrow morning early, François," she said. "Perhaps you will drive me into Nice before breakfast. I have some purchases to make."

He bowed and reached out his hand for the revolver which she had taken from him.

She looked at the ornate weapon, its silver-plated metal parts, the graceful ivory handle.

"I'm not going to trust you with this tonight," she said with her rare smile. "Goodnight, François."

He took her hand and kissed it.

"Goodnight, Jean," he said in a tremulous voice. For a moment their eyes met, and then she turned as though she dared not trust herself and followed her father down the stairs.

They were halfway to the house when she laid her hand on Briggerland's arm.

"Keep this," she said. It was François' revolver. "It is probably loaded and I thought I saw some silver initials inlaid in the ivory handle. If I know François Mordon, they are his."

"What do you want me to do with it?" he said as he slipped the weapon in his pocket.

She laughed.

"On your way to bed, come in to my room," she said. "I've quite a lot to tell you," and she sailed into the drawing-room to interrupt Mrs Cole-Mortimer, who was teaching a weary Lydia the elements of bezique.

"Where have you been, Jean?" asked Lydia, putting down her cards.

"I have been arranging a novel experience for you, but I'm not so sure that it will be as interesting as it might – it all depends upon the state of your young heart," said Jean, pulling up a chair.

"My young heart is very healthy," laughed Lydia. "What is the interesting experience?"

"Are you in love?" challenged Jean, searching in a big chintz bag where she kept her handiwork for a piece of unfinished sewing. (Jean's domesticity was always a source of wonder to Lydia.)

"In love – good heavens, no."

"So much the better," nodded Jean, "that sounds as though the experience will be fascinating."

She waited until she had threaded the fine needle before she explained.

"If you really are not in love and you sit on the Lovers' Chair, the name of your future husband will come to you. If you're in love, of course, that complicates matters a little."

"But suppose I don't want to know the name of my future husband?"

"Then you're inhuman," said Jean.

"Where is this magical chair?"

"It is on the San Remo road beyond the frontier station. You've been there, haven't you, Margaret?"

"Once," said Mrs Cole-Mortimer, who had not been east of Cap Martin, but whose rule it was never to admit that she had missed anything worth seeing.

"In a wild, eerie spot," Jean went on, "and miles from any human habitation."

"Are you going to take me?"

Jean shook her head.

"That would ruin the spell," she said solemnly. "No, my dear, if you want that thrill, and, seriously, it is worth while, because the scenery is the most beautiful of any along the coast, you must go alone."

Lydia nodded.

"I'll try it. Is it too far to walk?" she asked.

"Much too far," said Jean. "Mordon will drive you out. He knows the road very well and you ought not to take anybody but an experienced driver. I have a *permis* for the car to pass the frontier; you will probably meet father in San Remo – he is taking a motorcycle trip, aren't you, daddy?"

Mr Briggerland drew a long breath and nodded. He was beginning to understand.

34

There was lying in Monaco harbour a long white boat with a stumpy mast, which delighted in the name of *Jungle Queen*. It was the property of an impecunious English nobleman who made a respectable income from letting the vessel on hire.

Mrs Cole-Mortimer had seemed surprised at the reasonable fee demanded for two months' use until she had seen the boat the day after her arrival at Cap Martin.

She had pictured a large and commodious yacht; she found a reasonably sized motor launch with a whale-deck cabin. The description in the agent's catalogue that the *Jungle Queen* would "sleep four" was probably based on the experience of a party of young roisterers who had once hired the vessel. Supposing that the "four" were reasonably drunk or heavily drugged, it was possible for them to sleep on board the *Jungle Queen*. Normally two persons would have found it difficult, though by lying diagonally across the "cabin" one small-sized man could have slumbered without discomfort.

The *Jungle Queen* had been a disappointment to Jean also. Her busy brain had conceived an excellent way of solving her principal problem, but a glance at the *Jungle Queen* told her that the money she had spent on hiring the launch – and it was little better – was wasted. She herself hated the sea and had so little faith in the utility of the boat that she had even dismissed the youth who attended to its well-worn engines.

Mr Marcus Stepney, who was mildly interested in motor-boating, and considerably interested in any form of amusement which he could get at somebody else's expense, had so far been the sole patron of the *Jungle Queen*. It was his practice to take the boat out every morning for a two hours' sail, generally alone, though sometimes he would take somebody whose acquaintance he had made, and who was destined to be a source of profit to him in the future.

Jean's talk of the caveman method of wooing had made a big impression upon him, emphasised as it had been, and still was, by the two angry red scars across the back of his hand. Things were not going well with him; the supply of rich and trusting youths had suddenly dried up. The little games in his private sitting-room had dwindled to feeble proportions. He was still able to eke out a living, but his success at his private séances had been counterbalanced by heavy losses at the public tables.

It is a known fact that people who live outside the law keep to their own plane. The swindler very rarely commits acts of violence. The burglar who practises card-sharping as a sideline is virtually unknown.

Mr Stepney lived on a plausible tongue and a pair of highly dexterous hands. It had never occurred to him to go beyond his own sphere, and indeed violence was as repugnant to him as it was vulgar.

Yet the caveman suggestion appealed to him. He had a way with women of a certain kind, and if his confidence had been rather shaken by Jean's savagery and Lydia's indifference, he had not altogether abandoned the hope that both girls in their turn might be conquered by the adoption of the right method.

The method for dealing with Jean he had at the back of his mind.

As for Lydia – Jean's suggestion was very attractive. It was after a very heavily unprofitable night spent at the Nice Casino that he took his courage in both hands and drove to the Villa Casa.

He was an early arrival, but Lydia had already finished her *petit déjeuner* and she was painfully surprised to see him.

"I'm not swimming today, Mr Stepney," she said, "and you don't look as if you were either."

He was dressed in perfectly fitting white duck trousers, white shoes, and a blue nautical coat with brass buttons; a yachtsman's cap was set at an angle on his dark head.

"No, I'm going out to do a little fishing," he said, "and I was wondering whether, in your charity, you would accompany me."

She shook her head.

"I'm sorry – I have another engagement this morning," she said.

"Can't you break it?" he pleaded, "as an especial favour to me? I've made all preparations and I've got a lovely lunch on board – you said you would come fishing with me one day."

"I'd like to," she confessed, "but I really have something very important to do this morning."

She did not tell him that her important duty was to sit on the Lovers' Chair. Somehow her trip seemed just a little silly in the cold clear light of morning.

"I could have you back in time," he begged. "Do come along, Mrs Meredith! You're going to spoil my day."

"I'm sure Lydia wouldn't be so unkind."

Jean had made her appearance as they were speaking.

"What is the scheme, Lydia?"

"Mr Stepney wants me to go out in the yacht," said the girl, and Jean smiled.

"I'm glad you call it a 'yacht'," she said dryly. "You're the second person who has so described it. The first was the agent. Take her to-morrow, Marcus."

There was a glint of amusement in her eyes, and he felt that she knew what was at the back of his mind.

"All right," he said in a tone which suggested that it was anything but all right, and added, "I saw you flying through Nice this morning with that yellow-faced chauffeur of yours, Jean."

"Were you up so early?" she asked carelessly.

"I wasn't dressed, I was looking out of the window – my room faces the Promenade des Anglais. I don't like that fellow."

"I shouldn't let him know," said Jean coolly. "He is very sensitive. There are so many fellows that you dislike, too."

172

"I don't think you ought to allow him so much freedom," Marcus Stepney went on. He was not in an amiable frame of mind, and the knowledge that he was annoying the girl encouraged him. "If you give these French chauffeurs an inch they'll take a kilometre."

"I suppose they would," said Jean thoughtfully. "How is your poor hand, Marcus?"

He growled something under his breath and thrust his hand deep into the pocket of his reefer coat.

"It is quite well," he snapped, and went back to Monaco and his solitary boat trip, flaming.

"One of these days…" he muttered, as he tuned up the motor. He did not finish his sentence, but sent the nose of the *Jungle Queen* at full speed for the open sea.

Jean's talk with Mordon that morning had not been wholly satisfactory. She had calmed his suspicions to an extent, but he still harped upon the letter, and she had promised to give it to him that evening.

"My dear," she said, "you are too impulsive – too Gallic. I had a terrible scene with father last night. He wants me to break off the engagement; told me what my friends in London would say, and how I should be a social outcast."

"And you – you, Jean?" he asked.

"I told him that such things did not trouble me," she said, and her lips drooped sadly. "I know I cannot be happy with anybody but you, François, and I am willing to face the sneers of London, even the hatred and scorn of my father, for your sake."

He would have seized her hand, though they were in the open road, but she drew away from him.

"Be careful, Francois," she warned him. "Remember that you have a very little time to wait."

"I cannot believe my good fortune," he babbled, as he brought the car up the gentle incline into Monte Carlo. He dodged an early morning tram, missing an unsuspecting passenger, who had come round the back of the tramcar, by inches, and set the big Italia up the palm avenue into the town.

173

"It is incredible, and yet I always thought some great thing would happen to me, and, Jean, I have risked so much for you. I would have killed Madame in London if she had not been dragged out of the way by that old man, and did I not watch for you when the man Meredith – "

"Hush," she said in a low voice. "Let us talk about something else."

"Shall I see your father? I am sorry for what I did last night," he said when they were nearing the villa.

"Father has taken his motor bicycle and gone for a trip into Italy," she said. "No, I do not think I should speak to him, even if he were here. He may come round in time, François. You can understand that it is terribly distressing; he hoped I would make a great marriage. You must allow for father's disappointment."

He nodded. He did not drive her to the house, but stopped outside the garage.

"Remember, at half past ten you will take Madame Meredith to the Lovers' Chair – you know the place?"

"I know it very well," he said. "It is a difficult place to turn – I must take her almost into San Remo. Why does she want to go to the Lovers' Chair? I thought only the cheap people went there – "

"You must not tell her that," she said sharply. "Besides, I myself have been there."

"And who did you think of, Jean?" he asked suddenly.

She lowered her eyes.

"I will not tell you – now," she said, and ran into the house.

François stood gazing after her until she had disappeared, and then, like a man waking from a trance, he turned to the mundane business of filling his tank.

35

Lydia was dressing for her journey when Mrs Cole-Mortimer came into the saloon where Jean was writing.

"There's a telephone call from Monte Carlo," she said. "Somebody wants to speak to Lydia."

Jean jumped up.

"I'll answer it," she said.

The voice at the other end of the wire was harsh and unfamiliar to her.

"I want to speak to Mrs Meredith."

"Who is it?" asked Jean.

"It is a friend of hers," said the voice. "Will you tell her? The business is rather urgent."

"I'm sorry," said Jean, "but she's just gone out."

She heard an exclamation of annoyance. "Do you know where she's gone?" asked the voice.

"I think she's gone in to Monte Carlo," said Jean.

"If I miss her will you tell her not to go out again until I come to the house?"

"Certainly," said Jean politely, and hung up the telephone.

"Was that a call for me?"

It was Lydia's voice from the head of the stairs.

"Yes, dear. I think it was Marcus Stepney who wanted to speak to you. I told him you'd gone out," said Jean. "You didn't wish to speak to him?"

"Good heavens, no!" said Lydia. "You're sure you won't come with me?"

"I'd rather stay here," said Jean truthfully. The car was at the door, and Mordon, looking unusually spruce in his white dust coat, stood by the open door.

"How long shall I be away?" asked Lydia.

"About two hours, dear, you'll be very hungry when you come back," said Jean, kissing her. "Now, mind you think of the right man," she warned her in mockery.

"I wonder if I shall," said Lydia quietly.

Jean watched the car out of sight, then went back to the saloon. She was hardly seated before the telephone rang again, and she anticipated Mrs Cole-Mortimer, and answered it.

"Mrs Meredith has not gone in to Monte Carlo," said the voice. "Her car has not been seen on the road."

"Is that Mr Jaggs?" asked Jean sweetly.

"Yes, miss," was the reply.

"Mrs Meredith has come back now. I'm dreadfully sorry, I thought she had gone into Monte Carlo. She's in her room with a bad headache. Will you come and see her?"

There was an interval of silence. "Yes, I will come," said Jaggs. Twenty minutes later a taxicab set down the old man at the door, and a maid admitted him and brought him into the saloon.

Jean rose to meet him. She looked at the bowed figure of old Jaggs. Took him all in, from his iron-grey hair to his dusty shoes, and then she pointed to a chair.

"Sit down," she said, and old Jaggs obeyed. "You've something very important to tell Mrs Meredith, I suppose."

"I'll tell her that myself, miss," said the old man gruffly.

"Well, before you tell her anything, I want to make a confession," she smiled down on old Jaggs, and pulled up a chair so that she faced him.

He was sitting with his back to the light, holding his battered hat on his knees.

"I've really brought you up under false pretences," she said, "because Mrs Meredith isn't here at all."

"Not here?" he said, half rising.

"No, she's gone for a ride with our chauffeur. But I wanted to see you, Mr Jaggs, because – " she paused. "I realise that you're a dear friend of hers and have her best interests at heart. I don't know who you are," she said, shaking her head, "but I know, of course, that Mr John Glover has employed you."

"What's all this about?" he asked gruffly. "What have you to tell me?"

"I don't know how to begin," she said, biting her lips. "It is such a delicate matter that I hate talking about it at all. But the attitude of Mrs Meredith to our chauffeur Mordon is distressing, and I think Mr Glover should be told."

He did not speak and she went on.

"These things do happen, I know," she said, "but I am happy to say that nothing of that sort has come into my experience, and, of course, Mordon is a good-looking man and she is young – "

"What are you talking about?" His tone was dictatorial and commanding.

"I mean," she said, "that I fear poor Lydia is in love with Mordon."

He sprang to his feet.

"It's a damned lie!" he said, and she stared at him. "Now tell me what has happened to Lydia Meredith," he went on, "and let me tell you this, Jean Briggerland, that if one hair of that girl's head is harmed, I will finish the work I began out there," he pointed to the garden, "and strangle you with my own hands."

She lifted her eyes to his and dropped them again, and began to tremble, then turning suddenly on her heel, she fled to her room, locked the door and stood against it, white and shaking. For the second time in her life Jean Briggerland was afraid.

She heard his quick footsteps in the passage outside, and there came a tap on her door.

"Let me in," growled the man, and for a second she almost lost control of herself. She looked wildly round the room for some way of escape, and then as a thought struck her, she ran quickly into the bathroom, which opened from her room. A large sponge was set to dry by an open window, and this she seized; on a shelf by the side of the bath was a big bottle of ammonia, and averting her face, she poured its contents upon the sponge until it was sodden, then with the dripping sponge in her hand, she crept back, turned the key and opened the door.

The old man burst in, then, before he realised what was happening, the sponge was pressed against his face. The pungent drug almost blinded him, its paralysing fumes brought him on to his knees. He gripped her wrist and tried to press away her hand, but now her arm was round his neck, and he could not get the purchase.

With a groan of agony he collapsed on the floor. In that instant she was on him like a cat, her knee between his shoulders.

Half unconscious he felt his hands drawn to his back, and felt something lashing them together. She was using the silk girdle which had been about her waist, and her work was effective.

Presently she turned him over on his back. The ammonia was still in his eyes, and he could not open them. The agony was terrible, almost unendurable. With her hand under his arm he struggled to his feet. He felt her lead him somewhere, and suddenly he was pushed into a chair. She left him alone for a little while, but presently came back and began to tie his feet together. It was a most amazing single-handed capture – even Jean could never have imagined the ease with which she could gain her victory.

"I'm sorry to hurt an old man." There was a sneer in her voice which he had not heard before. "But if you promise not to shout, I will not gag you."

He heard the sound of running water, and presently with a wet cloth she began wiping his eyes gently.

"You will be able to see in a minute," said Jean's cool voice. "In the meantime you'll stay here until I send for the police."

For all his pain he was forced to chuckle.

"Until you send for the police, eh? You know me?"

"I only know you're a wicked old man who broke into this house whilst I was alone and the servants were out," she said.

"You know why I've come?" he insisted. "I've come to tell Mrs Meredith that a hundred thousand pounds have been taken from her bank on a forged signature."

"How absurd," said Jean. She was sitting on the edge of the bath looking at the bedraggled figure. "How could anybody draw money from Mrs Meredith's bank whilst her dear friend and guardian, Jack Glover, is in London to see that she is not robbed."

"Old Jaggs" glared up at her from his inflamed eyes.

"You know very well," he said distinctly, "that I am Jack Glover, and that I have not left Monte Carlo since Lydia Meredith arrived."

36

Mr Briggerland did not enthuse over any form of sport or exercise. His hobbies were confined to the handsome motorcycle, which not only provided him with recreation, but had, on occasion, been of assistance in the carrying out of important plans, formulated by his daughter.

He stopped at Menton for breakfast and climbed the hill to Grimaldi after passing the frontier station at Pont St Louis. He had all the morning before him, and there was no great hurry. At Ventimille he had a second breakfast, for the morning was keen and his appetite was good. He loafed through the little town, with a cigar between his teeth, bought some curios at a shop and continued his leisurely journey.

His objective was San Remo. There was a train at one o'clock which would bring him and his machine back to Monte Carlo, where it was his intention to spend the remainder of the afternoon. At Pont St Louis he had had a talk with the Customs Officer.

"No, m'sieur, there are very few travellers on the road in the morning," said the official. "It is not until late in the afternoon that the traffic begins. Times have changed on the Riviera, and so many people go to Cannes. The old road is almost now deserted."

At eleven o'clock Mr Briggerland came to a certain part of the road and found a hiding place for his motorcycle – a small plantation of olive trees on the hillside. Incidentally it was an admirable resting place, for from here he commanded an extensive view of the western road.

Lydia's journey had been no less enjoyable. She, too, had stopped at Menton to explore the town, and had left Pont St Louis an hour after Mr Briggerland had passed.

The road to San Remo runs under the shadow of steep hills through a bleak stretch of country from which even the industrious peasantry of northern Italy cannot win a livelihood. Save for isolated patches of cultivated land, the hills are bare and menacing.

With these gaunt plateaux on one side and the rock-strewn seashore on the other, there was little to hold the eye save an occasional glimpse of the Italian town in the far distance. There was a wild uncouthness about the scenery which awed the girl. Sometimes the car would be running so near the sea level that the spray of the waves hit the windows; sometimes it would climb over an out-jutting headland and she would look down upon a bouldered beach a hundred feet below.

It was on the crest of a headland that the car stopped.

Here the road ran out in a semicircle so that from where she sat she could not see its continuation either before or behind. Ahead it slipped round the shoulder of a high and overhanging mass of rock, through which the road must have been cut. Behind it dipped down to a cove, hidden from sight.

"There is the Lovers' Chair, mademoiselle," said Mordon.

Half a dozen feet beneath the road level was a broad shelf of rock. A few stone steps led down and she followed them. The Lovers' Chair was carved in the face of the rock and she sat down to view the beauty of the scene. The solitude, the stillness which only the lazy waves broke, the majesty of the setting, brought a strange peace to her. Beyond the edge of the ledge the cliff fell sheer to the water, and she shivered as she stepped back from her inspection.

Mordon did not see her go. He sat on the running board of his car, his pale face between his hands, a prey to his own gloomy thoughts. There must be a development, he told himself. He was beginning to get uneasy, and for the first time he doubted the sincerity of the woman who had been to him as a goddess.

He did not hear Mr Briggerland, for the dark man was light of foot, when he came round the shoulder of the hill. Mordon's back was toward him. Suddenly the chauffeur looked round.

"M'sieur," he stammered, and would have risen, but Briggerland laid his hand on his shoulder.

"Do not rise, François," he said pleasantly. "I am afraid I was hasty last night."

"M'sieur, it was I who was hasty," said Mordon huskily, "it was unpardonable…"

"Nonsense," Briggerland patted the man's shoulder. "What is that boat out there – a man o' war, François?"

François Mordon turned his head toward the sea, and Briggerland pointed the ivory-handled pistol he had held behind his back and shot him dead.

The report of the revolver thrown down by the rocks came to Lydia like a clap of thunder. At first she thought it was a tyre burst and hurried up the steps to see.

Mr Briggerland was standing with his back to the car. At his feet was the tumbled body of Mordon.

"Mr – Brig…!" she gasped, and saw the revolver in his hand. With a cry she almost flung herself down the steps as the revolver exploded. The bullet ripped her hat from her head, and she flung up her hands, thinking she had been struck.

Then the dark face showed over the parapet and again the revolver was presented. She stared for a second into his benevolent eyes, and then something hit her violently and she staggered back, and dropped over the edge of the shelf down, straight down into the sea below.

37

Probably Jean Briggerland never gave a more perfect representation of shocked surprise than when old Jaggs announced that he was Jack Glover.

"Mr Glover," she said incredulously. "If you'll be kind enough to release my hands," said Jack savagely, "I will convince you."

Jean, all meekness, obeyed, and presently he stood up with a groan.

"You've nearly blinded me," he said, turning to the glass.

"If I'd known it was you — "

"Don't make me laugh!" he snapped. "Of course you knew who it was!" He took off the wig and peeled the beard from his face.

"Was that very painful?" she asked. sympathetically, and Jack snorted.

"How was I to know that it was you?" she demanded, virtuously indignant, "I thought you were a wicked old man — "

"You thought nothing of the sort, Miss Briggerland," said Jack. "You knew who I was, and you guessed why I had taken on this disguise. I was not many yards from you when it suddenly dawned upon you that I could not sleep at Lydia Meredith's flat unless I went there in the guise of an old man."

"Why should you want to sleep at her flat at all?" she asked innocently. "It doesn't seem to me to be a very proper ambition."

"That is an unnecessary question, and I'm wasting my time when I answer you," said Jack sternly. "I went there to save her life, to protect her against your murderous plots!"

"My murderous plots?" she repeated aghast. "You surely don't know what you're saying."

"I know this," and his face was not pleasant to see. "I have sufficient evidence to secure the arrest of your father, and possibly yourself. For months I have been working on that first providential accident of yours – the rich Australian who died with such remarkable suddenness. I may not get you in the Meredith case, and I may not be able to jail you for your attacks on Mrs Meredith, but I have enough evidence to hang your father for the earlier crime."

Her face was blank – expressionless. Never before had she been brought up short with such a threat as the man was uttering, nor had she ever been in danger of detection. And all the time she was eyeing him so steadily, not a muscle of her face moving, her mind was groping back into the past, examining every detail of the crime he had mentioned, seeking for some flaw in the carefully prepared plan which had brought a good man to a violent and untimely end.

"That kind of bluff doesn't impress me," she said at last. "You're in a poor way when you have to invent crimes to attach to me."

"We'll go into that later. Where is Lydia?" he said shortly.

"I tell you I don't know, except that she has gone out for a drive. I expect her back very soon."

"Is your father with her?"

She shook her head.

"No, father went out early. I don't know who gave you authority to cross-examine me. Why, Jack Glover, you have all the importance of a French examining magistrate," she smiled.

"You may learn how important they are soon," he said significantly. "Where is your chauffeur, Mordon?"

"He is gone, too – in fact, he is driving Lydia. Why?" she asked with a little tightening of heart. She had only just been in time, she thought. So they had associated Mordon with the forgery!

His first words confirmed this suspicion.

"There is a warrant for Mordon which will be executed as soon as he returns," said Jack. "We have been able to trace him in London and also the woman who presented the cheque. We know his movements from the time he left Nice by aeroplane for Paris to the time he returned to Nice. The people who changed the money for him will swear to his identity."

If he expected to startle her he was disappointed. She raised her eyebrows.

"I can't believe it is possible. Mordon was such an honest man," she said. "We trusted him implicitly, and never once did he betray our trust. Now, Mr Glover," she said coolly, "might I suggest that an interview with a gentleman in my bedroom is not calculated to increase my servants' respect for me? Will you go downstairs and wait until I come?"

"You'll not attempt to leave this house?" he said, and she laughed.

"Really, you're going on like one of those infallible detectives one reads about in the popular magazines," she said a little contemptuously. "You have no authority whatever to keep me from leaving this house and nobody knows that better than you. But you needn't be afraid. Sit on the stairs if you like until I come down."

When he had gone she rang the bell for her maid and handed her an envelope.

"I shall be in the saloon, talking to Mr Glover," she said in a low voice. "I want you to bring this in and say that you found it in the hall."

"Yes, miss," said the woman.

Jean proceeded leisurely to her toilet. In the struggle her dress had been torn, and she changed it for a pale green silk gown, and Jack, pacing in the hall below, was on the point of coming up to discover if she had made her escape, when she sailed serenely down the stairs.

"I should like to know one thing, Mr Glover," she said as she went into the saloon. "What do you intend doing? What is your immediate plan? Are you going to spirit Lydia away from us? Of course, I know you're in love with her and all that sort of thing."

His face went pink.

"I am not in love with Mrs Meredith," he lied.

"Don't be silly," she said practically, "of course you're in love with her."

185

"My first job is to get that money back, and you're going to help me," he said.

"Of course I'm going to help you," she agreed. "If Mordon has been such a scoundrel, he must suffer the consequence. I'm sure that you are too clever to have made any mistake. Poor Mordon. I wonder what made him do it, because he is such a good friend of Lydia's, and seriously, Mr Glover, I do think Lydia is being indiscreet."

"You made that remark before," he said quietly. "Now perhaps you'll explain what you mean."

She shrugged her shoulders.

"They are always about together. I saw them strolling on the lawn last night till quite a late hour, and I was so scared lest Mrs Cole-Mortimer noticed it too – "

"Which means that Mrs Cole-Mortimer did not notice it. You're clever, Jean! Even as you invent you make preparations to refute any evidence that the other side can produce. I don't believe a word you say."

There was a knock at the door and the maid entered bearing a letter on a salver.

"This was addressed to you, miss," she said. "It was on the hall table – didn't you see it?"

"No," said Jean in surprise. She took the letter, looked down at the address and opened it.

He saw a look of amazement and horror come to her face.

"Good God!" gasped Jean.

"What is it?" he said, springing up.

She stared at the letter again and from the letter to him.

"Read it," she said in a hollow voice.

"Dear Mademoiselle,
"I have returned from London and have confessed to Madame Meredith that I have forged her name and have drawn £100,000 from her bank. And now I have learnt that Madame Meredith loves me. There is only one end to this – that which you see – "

Jack read the letter twice.

"It is in his writing, too," he muttered. "It's impossible, incredible! I tell you I've had Mrs Meredith under my eyes all the time she has been here. Is there a letter from her?" he asked suddenly. "But no, it is impossible, impossible!"

"I haven't been into her room. Will you come up with me?"

He followed her up the stairs and into Lydia's big bedroom, and the first thing that caught his eye was a sealed letter on a table near the bed. He picked it up. It was addressed to him, in Lydia's handwriting, and feverishly he tore it open.

His face, when he had finished reading, was as white as hers had been.

"Where have they gone?" he asked.

"They went to San Remo."

"By car?"

"Of course."

Without a word he turned and ran down the stairs out of the house.

The taxi that had brought him in the role of Jaggs had gone, but down the road, a dozen yards away, was the car he had hired on the day he came to Monte Carlo. He gave instructions to the driver and jumped in. The car sped through Menton, stopped only the briefest while at the Customs barrier whilst Jack pursued his inquiries.

Yes, a lady had passed, but she had not returned.

How long ago?

Perhaps an hour; perhaps less.

At top speed the big car thundered along the sea road, twisting and turning, diving into valleys and climbing steep headlands, and then rounding a corner, Jack saw the car and a little crowd about it. His heart turned to stone as he leapt to the road.

He saw the backs of two Italian gendarmes, and pushing aside the little knot of idlers, he came into the centre of the group and stopped. Mordon lay on his face in a pool of blood, and one of the policemen was holding an ivory-handled revolver.

"It was with this that the crime was committed," he said in florid Italian. "Three of the chambers are empty. Now, at whom were the other two discharged?"

Jack reeled and gripped the mud-guard of the car for support, then his eyes strayed to the opening in the wall which ran on the seaward side of the road.

He walked to the parapet and looked over, and the first thing he saw was a torn hat and veil, and he knew it was Lydia's.

38

Mr Briggerland, killing time on the quay at Monaco, saw the *Jungle Queen* come into harbour and watched Marcus land, carrying his lines in his hand.

As Marcus came abreast of him he called and Mr Stepney looked round with a start.

"Hello, Briggerland," he said, swallowing something.

"Well, have you been fishing?" asked Mr Briggerland in his most paternal manner.

"Yes," admitted Marcus. "Did you catch anything?"

Stepney nodded.

"Only one," he said.

"Hard luck," said Mr Briggerland, with a smile, "but where is Mrs Meredith – I understood she was going out with you today?"

"She went to San Remo," said Stepney shortly, and the other nodded.

"To be sure," he said. "I had forgotten that."

Later he bought a copy of the *Niçoise* and learnt of the tragedy on the San Remo road. It brought him back to the house, a visibly agitated man.

"This is shocking news, my dear," he panted into the saloon and stood stock still at the sight of Mr Jack Glover.

"Come in, Briggerland," said Jack, without ceremony. There was a man with him, a tall, keen Frenchman whom Briggerland recognised as the chief detective of the Préfecture. "We want you to give an account of your actions."

"My actions?" said Mr Briggerland indignantly. "Do you associate me with this dreadful tragedy? A tragedy," he said, "which has stricken me almost dumb with horror and remorse. Why did I ever allow that villain even to speak to poor Lydia?"

"Nevertheless, m'sieur," said the tall man quietly, "you must tell us where you have been."

"That is easily explained. I went to San Remo."

"By road?"

"Yes, by road," said Mr Briggerland, "on my motor bicycle."

"What time did you arrive in San Remo?"

"At midday, or it may have been a quarter of an hour before."

"You know that the murder must have been committed at half past eleven?" said Jack.

"So the newspapers tell me."

"Where did you go in San Remo?" asked the detective.

"I went to a café and had a glass of wine, then I strolled about the town and lunched at the Victoria. I caught the one o'clock train to Monte Carlo."

"Did you hear nothing of the murder?"

"Not a word," said Mr Briggerland, "not a word."

"Did you see the car?"

Mr Briggerland shook his head.

"I left some time before poor Lydia," he said softly.

"Did you know of any attachment between the chauffeur and your guest?"

"I had no idea such a thing existed. If I had," said Mr Briggerland virtuously, "I should have taken immediate steps to have brought poor Lydia to her senses."

"Your daughter says that they were frequently together. Did you notice this?"

"Yes, I did notice it, but my daughter and I are very democratic. We have made a friend of Mordon and I suppose what would have seemed familiar to you, would pass unnoticed with us. Yes, I certainly do remember my poor friend and Mordon walking together in the garden."

"Is this yours?" The detective took from behind a curtain an old British rifle.

"Yes, that is mine," admitted Briggerland without a moment's hesitation. "It is one I bought in Amiens, a souvenir of our gallant soldiers – "

"I know, I quite understand your patriotic motive in purchasing it," said the detective dryly, "but will you tell us how this passed from your possession."

"I haven't the slightest notion," said Mr Briggerland in surprise. "I had no idea it was lost – I'd lost sight of it for some weeks. Can it be that Mordon – but no, I must not think so evilly of him."

"What were you going to suggest?" asked Jack. "That Mordon fired at Mrs Meredith when she was on the swimming raft? If you are, I can save you the trouble of telling that lie. It was you who fired, and it was I who knocked you out."

Mr Briggerland's face was a study.

"I can't understand why you make such a wild and unfounded charge," he said gently. "Perhaps, my dear, you could elucidate this mystery."

Jean had not spoken since he entered. She sat bolt upright on a chair, her hands folded in her lap, her sad eyes fixed now upon Jack, now upon the detective. She shook her head.

"I know nothing about the rifle, and did not even know you possessed one," she said. "But please answer all their questions, father. I am as anxious as you are to get to the bottom of this dreadful tragedy. Have you told my father about the letters which were discovered?"

The detective shook his head.

"I have not seen your father until he arrived this moment," he said.

"Letters?" Mr Briggerland looked at his daughter. "Did poor Lydia leave a letter?"

She nodded.

"I think Mr Glover will tell you, father," she said. "Poor Lydia had an attachment for Mordon. It is very clear what happened. They went out today, never intending to return – "

"Mrs Meredith had no intention of going to the Lovers' Chair until you suggested the trip to her," said Jack quietly. "Mrs Cole-Mortimer is very emphatic on that point."

"Has the body been found?" asked Mr Briggerland.

"Nothing has been found but the chauffeur," said the detective.

After a few more questions he took Jack outside.

"It looks very much to me as though it were one of those crimes of passion which are so frequent in this country," he said. "Mordon was a Frenchman and I have been able to identify him by tattoo marks on his arm, as a man who has been in the hands of the police many times."

"You think there is no hope?"

The detective shrugged his shoulders.

"We are dragging the pool. There is very deep water under the rock, but the chances are that the body has been washed out to sea. There is clearly no evidence against these people, except yours. The letters might, of course, have been forged, but you say you are certain that the writing is Mrs Meredith's."

Jack nodded.

They were walking down the road towards the officers' waiting car, when Jack asked: "May I see that letter again?"

The detective took it from his pocket book and Jack stopped and scanned it.

"Yes, it is her writing," he said and then uttered an exclamation.

"Do you see that?"

He pointed eagerly to two little marks before the words "Dear friend".

"Quotation marks," said the detective, puzzled. "Why did she write that?"

"I've got it," said Jack. "The story! Mademoiselle Briggerland told me she was writing a story, and I remember she said she had writer's cramp. Suppose she dictated a portion of the story to Mrs Meredith, and suppose in that story there occurred this letter: Lydia would have put the quotation marks mechanically."

The detective took the letter from his hand.

"It is possible," he said. "The writing is very even – it shows no sign of agitation, and of course the character's initials might be 'L M'. It is an ingenious hypothesis, and not wholly improbable, but if this were a part of the story, there would be other sheets. Would you like me to search the house?"

Jack shook his head.

"She's much too clever to have them in the house," he said. "More likely she's put them in the fire."

"What fire?" asked the detective dryly. "These houses have no fires, they're central heated – unless she went to the kitchen."

"Which she wouldn't do," said Jack thoughtfully. "No, she'd burn them in the garden."

The detective nodded, and they returned to the house.

Jean, deep in conversation with her father, saw them reappear, and watched them as they walked slowly across the lawn toward the trees, their eyes fixed on the ground.

"What are they looking for?" she asked with a frown.

"I'll go and see," said Briggerland, but she caught his arm.

"Do you think they'll tell you?" she asked sarcastically.

She ran up to her own room and watched them from behind a curtain. Presently they passed out of sight to the other side of the house, and she went into Lydia's room and overlooked them from there. Suddenly she saw the detective stoop and pick up something from the ground, and her teeth set.

"The burnt story," she said. "I never dreamt they'd look for that."

It was only a scrap they found, but it was in Lydia's writing, and the pencil mark was clearly visible on the charred ashes.

" 'Laura Martin'," read the detective. " 'L M', and there are the words 'tragic' and 'remorse'."

From the remainder of the charred fragments they collected nothing of importance. Jean watched them disappear along the avenue, and went down to her father.

"I had a fright," she said.

"You look as if you've still got it," he said. He eyed her keenly.

She shook her head.

193

"Father, you must understand that this adventure may end disastrously. There are ninety-nine chances against the truth being known, but it is the extra chance that is worrying me. We ought to have settled Lydia more quietly, more naturally. There was too much melodrama and shooting, but I don't see how we could have done anything else – Mordon was very tiresome."

"Where did Glover come from?" asked Mr Briggerland.

"He's been here all the time," said the girl.

"What?"

She nodded.

"He was old Jaggs. I had an idea he was, but I was certain when I remembered that he had stayed at Lydia's flat."

He put down his teacup and wiped his lips with a silk handkerchief.

"I wish this business was over," he said fretfully. "It looks as if we shall have trouble."

"Of course we shall," she said coldly. "You didn't expect to get a fortune of six hundred thousand pounds without trouble, did you? I dare say we shall be suspected. But it takes a lot of suspicion to worry me. We'll be in calm water soon, for the rest of our lives."

"I hope so," he said without any great conviction.

Mrs Cole-Mortimer was prostrate and in bed, and Jean had no patience to see her.

She herself ordered the dinner, and they had finished when a visitor in the shape of Mr Marcus Stepney came in.

It was unusual of Marcus to appear at the dinner hour, except in evening dress, and she remarked the fact wonderingly.

"Can I have a word with you, Jean?" he asked.

"What is it, what is it?" asked Mr Briggerland testily. "Haven't we had enough mysteries?"

Marcus eyed him without favour.

"We'll have another one, if you don't mind," he said unpleasantly, and the girl, whose every sense was alert, picked up a wrap and walked into the garden, with Marcus following on her heels.

Ten minutes passed and they did not return, a quarter of an hour went by, and Mr Briggerland grew uneasy. He got up from his chair, put down his book, and was halfway across the room when the door opened and Jack Glover came in, followed by the detective.

It was the Frenchman who spoke.

"M'sieur Briggerland, I have a warrant from the Préfect of the Alpes Maritimes for your arrest."

"My arrest?" spluttered the dark man, his teeth chattering. "What – what is the charge?"

"The wilful murder of François Mordon," said the officer.

"You lie – you lie," screamed Briggerland. "I have no knowledge of any – " His words sank into a throaty gurgle, and he stared past the detective. Lydia Meredith was standing in the doorway.

39

The morning for Mr Stepney had been doubly disappointing; again and again he drew up an empty line, and at last he flung the tackle into the well of the launch.

"Even the damn fish won't bite," he said, and the humour of his remark cheered him. He was ten miles from the shore, and the blue coast was a dim, ragged line on the horizon. He pulled out a big luncheon basket from the cabin and eyed it with disfavour. It had cost him two hundred francs. He opened the basket, and at the sight of its contents was inclined to reconsider his earlier view that he had wasted his money, the more so since the *maître d'hôtel* had thoughtfully included two quart bottles of champagne.

Mr Marcus Stepney made a hearty meal, and by the time he had dropped an empty bottle into the sea, he was inclined to take a more cheerful view of life. He threw over the debris of the lunch, pushed the basket under one of the seats of the cabin, pulled up his anchor and started the engines running.

The sky was a brighter blue and the sea held a finer sparkle, and he was inclined to take a view of even Jean Briggerland, more generous than any he had held.

"Little devil," he smiled reminiscently, as he murmured the words.

He opened the second bottle of champagne in her honour – Mr Marcus Stepney was usually an abstemious man – and drank solemnly, if not soberly, her health and happiness. As the sun grew warmer he began to feel an unaccountable sleepiness. He was sober enough to know that to fall asleep in the middle of the ocean was to ask for trouble, and he set the bow of the *Jungle Queen* for the nearest beach, hoping to find a landing place.

He found something better as he skirted the shore. The sea and the weather had scooped out a big hollow under a high cliff, a hollow just big enough to take the *Jungle Queen* and deep and still enough to ensure her a safe anchorage. A rock barrier interposed between the breakers and this deep pool which the waves had hollowed in the stony floor of the ocean. As he dropped his anchor he disturbed a school of fish, and his angling instincts reawoke. He let down his line over the side, seated himself comfortable in one of the two big basket chairs, and was dozing comfortably…

It was the sound of a shot that woke him. It was followed by another, and a third. Almost immediately something dropped from the cliff, and fell with a mighty splash into the water.

Marcus was wide awake now, and almost sobered. He peered down into the clear depths, and saw a figure of a woman turning over and over. Then as it floated upwards it came on its back, and he saw the face. Without a moment's hesitation he dived into the water.

He would have been wiser if he had waited until she floated to the surface, for now he found a difficulty in regaining the boat. After a great deal of trouble, he managed to reach into the launch and pull out a rope, which he fastened round the girl's waist and drew tight to a small stanchion. Then he climbed into the boat himself, and pulled her after him.

He thought at first she was dead, but listening intently he heard the beating of her heart, and searched the luncheon basket for a small flask of liqueurs, which Alphonse, the head waiter, had packed. He put the bottle to her lips and poured a small quantity into her mouth. She choked convulsively, and presently opened her eyes.

"You're amongst friends," said Marcus unnecessarily.

She sat up and covered her face with her hands. It all came back to her in a flash, and the horror of it froze her blood.

"What has happened to you?" asked Marcus.

"I don't know exactly," she said faintly. And then: "Oh, it was dreadful, dreadful!"

Marcus Stepney offered her the flask of liqueurs, and when she shook her head, he helped himself liberally.

Lydia was conscious of a pain in her left shoulder. The sleeve was torn, and across the thick of the arm there was an ugly raw weal.

"It looks like a bullet mark to me," said Marcus Stepney, suddenly grave. "I heard a shot. Did somebody shoot at you?"

She nodded.

"Who?"

She tried to frame the word, but no sound came, and then she burst into a fit of weeping.

"Not Jean?" he asked hoarsely.

She shook her head.

"Briggerland?"

She nodded.

"Briggerland!" Mr Stepney whistled, and as he whistled he shivered. "Let's get out of here," he said. "We shall catch our death of cold. The sun will warm us up."

He started the engines going, and safely navigated the narrow passage to the open sea. He had to get a long way out before he could catch a glimpse of the road, then he saw the car, and a cycling policeman dismounting and bending over something. He put away his telescope and turned to the girl.

"This is bad, Mrs Meredith," he said. "Thank God I wasn't in it."

"Where are you taking me?" she asked.

"I'm taking you out to sea," said Marcus with a little smile. "Don't get scared, Mrs Meredith. I want to hear that story of yours, and if it is anything like what I fear, then it would be better for you that Briggerland thinks you are dead."

She told the story as far as she knew it and he listened, not interrupting, until she had finished.

"Mordon dead, eh? That's bad. But how on earth are they going to explain it? I suppose," he said with a smile, "you didn't write a letter saying that you were going to run away with the chauffeur?"

She sat up at this.

"I did write a letter," she said slowly. "It wasn't a real letter, it was in a story which Jean was dictating."

She closed her eyes.

"How awful," she said. "I can't believe it even now."

"Tell me about the story," said the man quickly.

"It was a story she was writing for a London magazine, and her wrist hurt, and I wrote it down as she dictated. Only about three pages, but one of the pages was a letter supposed to have been written by the heroine saying that she was going away, as she loved somebody who was beneath her socially."

"Good God!" said Marcus, genuinely shocked. "Did Jean do that?"

He seemed absolutely crushed by the realisation of Jean Briggerland's deed, and he did not speak again for a long time.

"I'm glad I know," he said at last.

"Do you really think that all this time she has been trying to kill me?"

He nodded.

"She has used everybody, even me," he said bitterly. "I don't want you to think badly of me, Mrs Meredith, but I'm going to tell you the truth. I'd provisioned this little yacht today for a twelve hundred mile trip, and you were to be my companion."

"I?" she said incredulously.

"It was Jean's idea, really, though I think she must have altered her view, or thought I had forgotten all she suggested. I intended taking you out to sea and keeping you out there until you agreed – " he shook his head. "I don't think I could have done it really," he said, speaking half to himself. "I'm not really built for a conspirator. None of that rough stuff ever appealed to me. Well, I didn't try, anyway."

"No, Mr Stepney," she said quietly, "and I don't think, if you had, you would have succeeded."

He was in his frankest mood, and startled her later when he told her of his profession, without attempting to excuse or minimise the method by which he earned his livelihood.

"I was in a pretty bad way, and I thought there was easy money coming, and that rather tempted me," he said. "I know you will think I am a despicable cad, but you can't think too badly of me, really."

He surveyed the shore. Ahead of them the green tongue of Cap Martin jutted out into the sea.

"I think I'll take you to Nice," he said. "We'll attract less attention there, and probably I'll be able to get into touch with your old Mr Jaggs. You've no idea where I can find him? At any rate, I can go to the Villa Casa and discover what sort of a yarn is being told."

"And probably I can get my clothes dry," she said with a little grimace. "I wonder if you know how uncomfortable I am?"

"Pretty well," he said calmly. "Every time I move a new stream of water runs down my back."

It was half past three in the afternoon when they reached Nice, and Marcus saw the girl safely to an hotel, changed himself and brought the yacht back to Monaco, where Briggerland had seen him.

For two hours Marcus Stepney wrestled with his love for a girl who was plainly a murderess, and in the end love won. When darkness fell he provisioned the *Jungle Queen*, loaded her with petrol, and heading her out to sea made the swimming cove of Cap Martin. It was to the boat that Jean flew.

"What about my father?" she asked as she stepped aboard.

"I think they've caught him," said Marcus.

"He'll hate prison," said the girl complacently. "Hurry, Marcus, I'd hate it, too!"

40

Lydia took up her quarters in a quiet hotel in Nice and Mrs Cole-Mortimer agreed to stay on and chaperon her.

Though she had felt no effects from her terrifying experience on the first day, she found herself a nervous wreck when she woke in the morning, and wisely decided to stay in bed.

Jack, who had expected the relapse, called in a doctor, but Lydia refused to see him. The next day she received the lawyer.

She had only briefly outlined the part which Marcus Stepney had played in her rescue, but she had said enough to make Jack call at Stepney's hotel to thank him in person. Mr Stepney, however, was not at home – he had not been home all night, but this information his discreet informant did not volunteer. Nor was the disappearance of the *Jungle Queen* noticed for two days. It was Mrs Cole-Mortimer, in settling up her accounts with Jack, who mentioned the "yacht".

"The *Jungle Queen*," said Jack, "that's the motor launch, isn't it? I've seen her lying in the harbour. I thought she was Stepney's property."

His suspicions aroused, he called again at Stepney's hotel, and this time his inquiry was backed by the presence of a detective. Then it was made known that Mr Stepney had not been seen since the night of Briggerland's arrest.

"That is where they've gone. Stepney was very keen on the girl, I think," said Jack.

The detective was annoyed.

"If I'd known before we could have intercepted them. We have several destroyers in the harbour at Villafrance. Now I am afraid it is too late."

"Where would they make for?" asked Jack.

The officer shrugged his shoulders.

"God knows," he said. "They could get into Italy or into Spain, possibly Barcelona. I will telegraph the Chief of the Police there."

But the Barcelona police had no information to give. The *Jungle Queen* had not been sighted. The weather was calm, the sea smooth, and everything favourable for the escape.

Inquiries elicited the fact that Mr Stepney had bought large quantities of petrol a few days before his departure, and had augmented his supply the evening he had left. Also he had bought provisions in considerable quantities.

The murder was a week old, and Mr Briggerland had undergone his preliminary examination, when a wire came through from the Spanish police that a motor boat answering the description of the *Jungle Queen* had called at Malaga, had provisioned, refilled, and put out to sea again, before the police authorities, who had a description of the pair, had time to investigate.

"You'll think I have a diseased mind," said Lydia, "but I hope she gets away."

Jack laughed.

"If you had been with her much longer, Lydia, she would have turned you into a first-class criminal," he said. "I hope you do not forget that she has exactly a hundred thousand pounds of yours – in other words, a sixth of your fortune."

Lydia shook her head.

"That is almost a comforting thought," she said. "I know she is what she is, Jack, but her greatest crime is that she was born six hundred years too late. If she had lived in the days of the Italian Renaissance she would have made history."

"Your sympathy is immoral," said Jack. "By the way, Briggerland has been handed over to the Italian authorities. The crime was committed on Italian soil and that saves his head from falling into the basket."

She shuddered.

"What will they do to him?"

"He'll be imprisoned for life," was the reply "and I rather think that's a little worse than the guillotine. You say you worry for Jean – I'm rather sorry for old man Briggerland. If he hadn't tried to live up to his daughter he might have been a most respectable member of society."

They were strolling through the quaint, narrow streets of Grasse, and Jack, who knew and loved the town, was showing her sights which made her forget that the Perfumerie Factory, the Mecca of the average tourist, had any existence.

"I suppose I'll have to settle down now," she said with an expression of distaste.

"I suppose you will," said Jack, "and you'll have to settle up, too; your legal expenses are something fierce."

"Why do you say that?" she asked, stopping in her walk and looking at him gravely.

"I am speaking as your mercenary lawyer," said Jack.

"You are trying to put your service on another level," she corrected. "I owe everything I have to you. My fortune is the least of these. I owe you my life three times over."

"Four," he corrected, "and to Marcus Stepney once."

"Why have you done so much for me? Were you interested?" she asked after a pause.

"Very," he replied. "I was interested in you from the moment I saw you step out of Mr Mordon's taxi into the mud, but I was especially interested in you – "

"When?" she asked.

"When I sat outside your door night after night and discovered you didn't snore," he said shamelessly, and she went red.

"I hope you'll never refer to your old Jaggs' adventures. It was very – "

"What?"

"I was going to say horrid, but I shouldn't be telling the truth," she admitted frankly. "I liked having you there. Poor Mrs Morgan will be disconsolate when she discovers that we've lost our lodger."

They walked into the cool of the ancient cathedral and sat down.

"There's something very soothing about a church, isn't there?" he whispered. "Look at that gorgeous window. If I were ever rich enough to marry the woman I loved, I should be married in a cathedral like this, full of old tombs and statues and stained glass."

"How rich would you have to be?" she asked.

"As rich as she is."

She bent over toward him, her lips against his ear.

"Tell me how much money you have," she whispered, "and I'll give away all I have in excess of that amount."

He caught her hand and held it fast, and they sat there before the altar of St Catherine until the sun went down and the disapproving old woman who acted as the cathedral's caretaker tapped them on the shoulder.

41

"That is Gibraltar," said Marcus Stepney, pointing ahead to a grey shape that loomed up from the sea.

He was unshaven for he had forgotten to bring his razor and he was pinched with the cold. His overcoat was turned up to his ears, in spite of which he shivered.

Jean did not seem to be affected by the sudden change of temperature. She sat on the top of the cabin, her chin in the palm of her hand, her elbow on her crossed knee.

"You are not going into Gibraltar?" she asked.

He shook his head.

"I think not," he said, "nor to Algeciras. Did you see that fellow on the quay yelling for the craft to come back after we left Malaga? That was a bad sign. I expect the police have instructions to detain this boat, and most of the ports must have been notified."

"How long can we run?"

"We've got enough gas and grub to reach Dacca," he said. "That's roughly an eight days' journey."

"On the African coast?"

He nodded, although she could not see him.

"Where could we get a ship to take us to South America?" she asked, turning round.

"Lisbon," he said thoughtfully. "Yes, we could reach Lisbon, but there are too many steamers about and we're certain to be sighted. We might run across to Las Palmas, most of the South American boats call there, but if I were you I should stick to Europe. Come and take this helm, Jean."

She obeyed without question, and he continued the work which had been interrupted by a late meal, the painting of the boat's hull, a difficult business, involving acrobatics, since it was necessary for him to lean over the side. He had bought the grey paint at Malaga, and happily there was not much surface that required attention. The stumpy mast of the *Jungle Queen* had already gone overboard – he had sawn it off with great labour the day after they had left Cap Martin.

She watched him with a speculative eye as he worked, and thought he had never looked quite so unattractive as he did with an eight-days' growth of beard, his shirt stained with paint and petrol. His hands were grimy and nobody would have recognised in this scarecrow the elegant habitué of those fashionable resorts which smart society frequents.

Yet she had reason to be grateful to him. His conduct toward her had been irreproachable. Not one word of love had been spoken, nor, until now, had their future plans, for it affected them both, been discussed.

"Suppose we reach South America safely?" she asked. "What happens then, Marcus?"

He looked round from his work in surprise.

"We'll get married," he said quietly, and she laughed.

"And what happens to the present Mrs Stepney?"

"She has divorced me," said Stepney unexpectedly. "I got the papers the day we left."

"I see," said Jean softly. "We'll get married – " then stopped.

He looked at her and frowned.

"Isn't that your idea, too?" he asked.

"Married? Yes, that's my idea, too. It seems a queer uninteresting way of finishing things, doesn't it, and yet I suppose it isn't."

He had resumed his work and was leaning far over the bow intent upon his labour. Suddenly she spun the wheel round and the launch heeled over to starboard. For a second it seemed that Marcus Stepney could not maintain his balance against that unexpected impetus, but by a superhuman effort he kicked himself back to safety, and stared at her with a blanched face.

"Why did you do that?" he asked hoarsely. "You nearly had me overboard."

"There was a porpoise lying on the surface of the sea, asleep, I think," she said quietly. "I'm very sorry, Marcus, but I didn't know that it would throw you off your balance."

He looked round for the sleeping fish but it had disappeared.

"You told me to avoid them, you know," she said apologetically. "Did I really put you in any danger?"

He licked his dry lips, picked up the paint pot, and threw it into the sea.

"We'll leave this," he said, "until we are beached. You gave me a scare, Jean."

"I'm dreadfully sorry. Come here, and sit by me."

She moved to allow him room, and he sat down by her, taking the wheel from her hand.

On the horizon the high lands of northern Africa were showing their saw-edge outlines.

"That is Morocco," he pointed out to her. "I propose giving Gibraltar a wide berth, and following the coast line to Tangier."

"Tangier wouldn't be a bad place to land if there weren't two of us," he went on. "It is our being together in this yacht that is likely to cause suspicion. You could easily pretend that you'd come over from Gibraltar, and the port authorities there are pretty slack."

"Or if we could land on the coast," he suggested. "There's a good landing, and we could follow the beach down, and turn up in Tangier in the morning – all sorts of oddments turn up in Tangier without exciting suspicion."

She was looking out over the sea with a queer expression in her face.

"Morocco!" she said softly. "Morocco – I hadn't thought of that!"

They had a fright soon after. A grey shape came racing out of the darkening east, and Stepney put his helm over as the destroyer smashed past on her way to Gibraltar.

He watched the stern light disappearing, then it suddenly turned and presented its side to them.

"They're looking for us," said Marcus.

The darkness had come down, and he headed straight for the east.

There was no question that the destroyer was on an errand of discovery. A white beam of light shot out from her decks, and began to feel along the sea. And then when they thought it had missed them, it dropped on the boat and held. A second later it missed them and began a search. Presently it lit the little boat, and it did something more – it revealed a thickening of the atmosphere. They were running into a sea fog, one of those thin white fogs that come down in the Mediterranean on windless days. The blinding glare of the searchlight blurred.

"Bang!"

"That's the gun to signal us to stop," said Marcus between his teeth.

He turned the nose of the boat southward, a hazardous proceeding, for he ran into clear water, and had only just got back into the shelter of the providential fog bank when the white beam came stealthily along the edge of the mist. Presently it died out, and they saw it no more.

"They're looking for us," said Marcus again.

"You said that before," said the girl calmly.

"They've probably warned them at Tangier. We dare not take the boat into the bay," said Stepney, whose nerves were now on edge.

He turned again westward, edging toward the rocky coast of northern Africa. They saw little clusters of lights on the shore, and he tried to remember what towns they were.

"I think that big one is Cutra, the Spanish convict station," he said.

He slowed down the boat, and they felt their way gingerly along the coast line, until the flick and flash of a lighthouse gave them an idea of their position.

"Cape Spartel," he identified the light. "We can land very soon. I was in Morocco for three months, and if I remember rightly the beach is good walking as far as Tangier."

She went into the cabin and changed, and as the nose of the *Jungle Queen* slid gently up the sandy beach she was ready.

He carried her ashore, and set her down, then he pushed off the nose of the boat, and manoeuvred it so that the stern was against the beach, resting in three feet of water. He jumped on board, lashed the helm, and started the engines going, then wading back to the shore he stood staring into the gloom as the little *Jungle Queen* put out to sea.

"That's that," he said grimly. "Now my dear, we've got a ten-mile walk before us."

But he had made a slight miscalculation. The distance between himself and Tangier was twenty-five miles, and involved several detours inland into country which was wholly uninhabited, save at that moment it held the camp of Muley Hafiz, who was engaged in negotiation with the Spanish Government for one of those "permanent peaces" which frequently last for years.

Muley Hafiz sat drinking his coffee at midnight, listening to the strains of an ornate gramophone, which stood in a corner of his square tent.

A voice outside the silken fold of his tent greeted him, and he stopped the machine.

"What is it?" he asked.

"Lord, we have captured a man and a woman walking along by the sea."

"They are Riffi people – let them go," said Muley in Arabic. "We are making peace, my man, not war."

"Lord, these are infidels; I think they are English."

Muley Hafiz twisted his trim little beard.

"Bring them," he said.

So they were brought to his presence, a dishevelled man and a girl at the sight of whose face he gasped.

"My little friend of the Riviera," he said wonderingly, and the smile she gave him was like a ray of sunshine to his heart.

He stood up, a magnificent figure of a man, and she eyed him admiringly.

"I am sorry if my men have frightened you," he said. "You have nothing to fear, madame. I will send my soldiers to escort you to Tangier."

And then he frowned. "Where did you come from?"

She could not lie under the steady glance of those liquid eyes.

"We landed on the shore from a boat. We lost our way," she said. He nodded.

"You must be she they are seeking," he said. "One of my spies came to me from Tangier tonight, and told me that the Spanish and the French police were waiting to arrest a lady who had committed some crime in France. I cannot believe it is you – or if it is, then I should say the crime was pardonable."

He glanced at Marcus.

"Or perhaps," he said slowly, "it is your companion they desire."

Jean shook her head.

"No, they do not want him," she said, "it is I they want."

He pointed to a cushion.

"Sit down," he said, and followed her example.

Marcus alone remained standing, wondering how this strange situation would develop.

"What will you do? If you go into Tangier I fear I could not protect you, but there is a city in the hills," he waved his hand, "many miles from here, a city where the hills are green, mademoiselle, and where beautiful springs gush out of the ground, and there I am lord."

She drew a long breath.

"I will go to the city of the hills," she said softly, "and this man," she shrugged her shoulders, "I do not care what happens to him," she said, with a smile of amusement at the pallid Marcus.

"Then he shall go to Tangier alone."

But Marcus Stepney did not go alone. For the last two miles of the journey he had carried a bag containing the greater part of five million francs that the girl had brought from the boat. Jean did not remember this until she was on her way to the city of the hills, and by that time money did not interest her.

Edgar Wallace

Big Foot

Footprints and a dead woman bring together Superintendent Minton and the amateur sleuth Mr Cardew. Who is the man in the shrubbery? Who is the singer of the haunting Moorish tune? Why is Hannah Shaw so determined to go to Pawsy, 'a dog lonely place' she had previously detested? Death lurks in the dark and someone must solve the mystery before BIG FOOT strikes again, in a yet more fiendish manner.

Bones In London

The new Managing Director of Schemes Ltd has an elegant London office and a theatrically dressed assistant – however Bones, as he is better known, is bored. Luckily there is a slump in the shipping market and it is not long before Joe and Fred Pole pay Bones a visit. They are totally unprepared for Bones' unnerving style of doing business, unprepared for his unique style of innocent and endearing mischief.

EDGAR WALLACE

BONES OF THE RIVER

'Taking the little paper from the pigeon's leg, Hamilton saw it was from Sanders and marked URGENT. *Send Bones instantly to Lujamalababa… Arrest and bring to head-quarters the witch doctor.*'

It is a time when the world's most powerful nations are vying for colonial honour, a time of trading steamers and tribal chiefs. In the mysterious African territories administered by Commissioner Sanders, Bones persistently manages to create his own unique style of innocent and endearing mischief.

THE DAFFODIL MYSTERY

When Mr Thomas Lyne, poet, poseur and owner of Lyne's Emporium insults a cashier, Odette Rider, she resigns. Having summoned detective Jack Tarling to investigate another employee, Mr Milburgh, Lyne now changes his plans. Tarling and his Chinese companion refuse to become involved. They pay a visit to Odette's flat. In the hall Tarling meets Sam, convicted felon and protégé of Lyne. Next morning Tarling discovers a body. The hands are crossed on the breast, adorned with a handful of daffodils.

Edgar Wallace

The Joker

While the millionaire Stratford Harlow is in Princetown, not only does he meet with his lawyer Mr Ellenbury but he gets his first glimpse of the beautiful Aileen Rivers, niece of the actor and convicted felon Arthur Ingle. When Aileen is involved in a car accident on the Thames Embankment, the driver is James Carlton of Scotland Yard. Later that evening Carlton gets a call. It is Aileen. She needs help.

The Square Emerald

'Suicide on the left,' says Chief Inspector Coldwell pleasantly, as he and Leslie Maughan stride along the Thames Embankment during a brutally cold night. A gaunt figure is sprawled across the parapet. But Coldwell soon discovers that Peter Dawlish, fresh out of prison for forgery, is not considering suicide but murder. Coldwell suspects Druze as the intended victim. Maughan disagrees. If Druze dies, she says, 'It will be because he does not love children!'

OTHER TITLES BY EDGAR WALLACE AVAILABLE DIRECT
FROM HOUSE OF STRATUS

Quantity		£	$(US)	$(CAN)	€
☐	THE ADMIRABLE CARFEW	6.99	11.50	15.99	11.50
☐	THE AVENGER	6.99	11.50	15.99	11.50
☐	BARBARA ON HER OWN	6.99	11.50	15.99	11.50
☐	BIG FOOT	6.99	11.50	15.99	11.50
☐	THE BLACK ABBOT	6.99	11.50	15.99	11.50
☐	BONES	6.99	11.50	15.99	11.50
☐	BONES IN LONDON	6.99	11.50	15.99	11.50
☐	BONES OF THE RIVER	6.99	11.50	15.99	11.50
☐	THE CLUE OF THE NEW PIN	6.99	11.50	15.99	11.50
☐	THE CLUE OF THE SILVER KEY	6.99	11.50	15.99	11.50
☐	THE CLUE OF THE TWISTED CANDLE	6.99	11.50	15.99	11.50
☐	THE COAT OF ARMS	6.99	11.50	15.99	11.50
☐	THE COUNCIL OF JUSTICE	6.99	11.50	15.99	11.50
☐	THE CRIMSON CIRCLE	6.99	11.50	15.99	11.50
☐	THE DAFFODIL MYSTERY	6.99	11.50	15.99	11.50
☐	THE DARK EYES OF LONDON	6.99	11.50	15.99	11.50
☐	THE DAUGHTERS OF THE NIGHT	6.99	11.50	15.99	11.50
☐	A DEBT DISCHARGED	6.99	11.50	15.99	11.50
☐	THE DEVIL MAN	6.99	11.50	15.99	11.50
☐	THE DOOR WITH SEVEN LOCKS	6.99	11.50	15.99	11.50
☐	THE DUKE IN THE SUBURBS	6.99	11.50	15.99	11.50
☐	THE FACE IN THE NIGHT	6.99	11.50	15.99	11.50
☐	THE FEATHERED SERPENT	6.99	11.50	15.99	11.50
☐	THE FLYING SQUAD	6.99	11.50	15.99	11.50
☐	THE FORGER	6.99	11.50	15.99	11.50
☐	THE FOUR JUST MEN	6.99	11.50	15.99	11.50
☐	FOUR SQUARE JANE	6.99	11.50	15.99	11.50
☐	THE FOURTH PLAGUE	6.99	11.50	15.99	11.50

ALL HOUSE OF STRATUS BOOKS ARE AVAILABLE FROM GOOD BOOKSHOPS
OR DIRECT FROM THE PUBLISHER:

Internet: www.houseofstratus.com including author interviews, reviews, features.

Email: sales@houseofstratus.com please quote author, title and credit card details.

OTHER TITLES BY EDGAR WALLACE AVAILABLE DIRECT FROM HOUSE OF STRATUS

Quantity		£	$(US)	$(CAN)	€
	THE FRIGHTENED LADY	6.99	11.50	15.99	11.50
	GOOD EVANS	6.99	11.50	15.99	11.50
	THE HAND OF POWER	6.99	11.50	15.99	11.50
	THE IRON GRIP	6.99	11.50	15.99	11.50
	THE JOKER	6.99	11.50	15.99	11.50
	THE JUST MEN OF CORDOVA	6.99	11.50	15.99	11.50
	THE KEEPERS OF THE KING'S PEACE	6.99	11.50	15.99	11.50
	THE LAW OF THE FOUR JUST MEN	6.99	11.50	15.99	11.50
	THE LONE HOUSE MYSTERY	6.99	11.50	15.99	11.50
	THE MAN WHO BOUGHT LONDON	6.99	11.50	15.99	11.50
	THE MAN WHO KNEW	6.99	11.50	15.99	11.50
	THE MAN WHO WAS NOBODY	6.99	11.50	15.99	11.50
	THE MIND OF MR J G REEDER	6.99	11.50	15.99	11.50
	MORE EDUCATED EVANS	6.99	11.50	15.99	11.50
	MR J G REEDER RETURNS	6.99	11.50	15.99	11.50
	MR JUSTICE MAXWELL	6.99	11.50	15.99	11.50
	RED ACES	6.99	11.50	15.99	11.50
	ROOM 13	6.99	11.50	15.99	11.50
	SANDERS	6.99	11.50	15.99	11.50
	SANDERS OF THE RIVER	6.99	11.50	15.99	11.50
	THE SINISTER MAN	6.99	11.50	15.99	11.50
	THE SQUARE EMERALD	6.99	11.50	15.99	11.50
	THE THREE JUST MEN	6.99	11.50	15.99	11.50
	THE THREE OAK MYSTERY	6.99	11.50	15.99	11.50
	THE TRAITOR'S GATE	6.99	11.50	15.99	11.50
	WHEN THE GANGS CAME TO LONDON	6.99	11.50	15.99	11.50
	WHEN THE WORLD STOPPED	6.99	11.50	15.99	11.50

Hotline: UK ONLY: **0800 169 1780**, please quote author, title and credit card details.
INTERNATIONAL: **+44 (0) 20 7494 6400**, please quote author, title and credit card details.

Send to: **House of Stratus Sales Department**
24c Old Burlington Street
London
W1X 1RL
UK

Please allow for postage costs charged per order plus an amount per book as set out in the tables below:

	£(Sterling)	$(US)	$(CAN)	€(Euros)
Cost per order				
UK	2.00	3.00	4.50	3.30
Europe	3.00	4.50	6.75	5.00
North America	3.00	4.50	6.75	5.00
Rest of World	3.00	4.50	6.75	5.00
Additional cost per book				
UK	0.50	0.75	1.15	0.85
Europe	1.00	1.50	2.30	1.70
North America	2.00	3.00	4.60	3.40
Rest of World	2.50	3.75	5.75	4.25

PLEASE SEND CHEQUE, POSTAL ORDER (STERLING ONLY), EUROCHEQUE, OR INTERNATIONAL MONEY ORDER (PLEASE CIRCLE METHOD OF PAYMENT YOU WISH TO USE)
MAKE PAYABLE TO: STRATUS HOLDINGS plc

Cost of book(s): ————— Example: 3 x books at £6.99 each: £20.97

Cost of order: ————— Example: £2.00 (Delivery to UK address)

Additional cost per book: ————— Example: 3 x £0.50: £1.50

Order total including postage: ————— Example: £24.47

Please tick currency you wish to use and add total amount of order:

☐ £ (Sterling)   ☐ $ (US)   ☐ $ (CAN)   ☐ € (EUROS)

VISA, MASTERCARD, SWITCH, AMEX, SOLO, JCB:

☐☐☐☐☐☐☐☐☐☐☐☐☐☐☐☐☐☐☐☐☐☐

Issue number (Switch only):
☐☐☐

Start Date: **Expiry Date:**
☐☐/☐☐   ☐☐/☐☐

Signature: ——————————

NAME: ——————————————————————

ADDRESS: ——————————————————————

——————————————————————

POSTCODE: ——————

Please allow 28 days for delivery.

Prices subject to change without notice.
Please tick box if you do not wish to receive any additional information. ☐

House of Stratus publishes many other titles in this genre; please check our website (**www.houseofstratus.com**) for more details.